Deceptive Images

Joanne Henning

J.D. Henning

Cover design: Rebecca Finkel, FPGD.com

A special thanks to the wonderful dance instructors who have filled my life with joy and grace. You are the inspiration for this story.

Prologue 1972

The summer of 1972 was a turning point in Rosa Fletcher's life. The road trip with her high school friend, Angelica, was supposed to be a week of fun and horseback riding, but Rosa's touching memories of that summer vacation lingered and resonated into adulthood. It all began on a perfect evening in July.

The scenery in the Adirondacks was stunning. Rosa traveled with Angelica's parents, Mr. and Mrs. D'Augelli. As they neared their destination, the air was crisp and clean; the atmosphere, magical. A full moon peeked in and out of the cloud cover as they passed a myriad of lakes, and the moonlight sparkled on the calm waters. The car windows were open as they savored the fresh forest scent of pine and experienced a thrilling sense of adventure. When they arrived, they found a ranch nestled in the wilderness with a large private lake as its focal point and checked into a rustic two-bedroom cabin with a lake view. The girls opened the windows, unpacked their suitcases, and stretched out on the twin beds that were so comfortable after the long drive. They tried to temper their excitement and get some sleep. The first riding lesson was early in the morning.

Rosa and Angelica had breakfast while Mr. and Mrs. D'Augelli slept in. Angelica's parents were not early risers. Rosa, amused they chose a ranch for their vacation, thought Mrs. D'Augelli was glamorous and not the type to get on a horse. Her husband was there on the whim of his wife and daughter and would be more comfortable in the city or at a casino. He hoped to find a group of men who played cards. Even Rosa wondered what she was doing at the ranch. She liked horses, but the thought of riding one was terrifying. Rosa cringed when she remembered giving the horses sugar cubes when visiting her uncle in the country. She was certain it was bad for their teeth. She hovered behind Angelica when they arrived at the lesson, while Cal, the cowboy in charge, zeroed in on the anxiety of his new pupil.

"Are you planning to ride today?" he asked quietly as he approached Rosa.

She hesitated. "I think so."

He smiled. "Don't worry, I will fix you up with Snowball, the sweetest, gentlest horse in the stable." He put her at ease by calling her "Rosie" and called Angelica "Angie". The cowboys used these nicknames for the girls the rest of the week, and had adopted descriptive Western names like Cal, Curly, Lindy, Wyatt, and Russ. The teasing and nicknames were all good-natured fun, and Rosa felt more comfortable attending the lesson. Afterward, Rosa and Angelica swam and enjoyed group activities in the afternoon.

Before dinner, Angelica prepared for a night out. Rosa worried she didn't have the right clothes and suspected her friend Angelica was more interested in meeting boys than riding horses. Rosa took a walk to be by herself, overwhelmed with plans for the evening. She settled under a shade tree, opened her novel, and savored the solitude and the cool country breeze. A conversation in the barn interrupted her reverie.

"So there are a lot of single ladies in the group," said Cal, "so let's make sure they feel welcomed."

"No problem," bragged Lindy. He was a ladies' man.

"And Curly, make sure those two young girls get your attention. They're around your age."

"The shorter one is a little too bold for me, and I'd rather not encourage her," said Curly. "I think that could be trouble."

"Focus on the other one."

Rosa thought she would die; they were talking about her. She had to disappear before they realized she could hear them. She was sixteen and not yet ready for flirtations with older guys.

When they returned to the clubhouse that night, Angelica met a boy from college. Rosa towered over his friend, but he politely danced with her. She suspected he would prefer a dance partner more his height. The band played until 2 am, and the girls stayed until closing.

The next day, Rosa rode a different horse named Jack. Curly was the cowboy teaching the group. Rosa's heart did a little flip when she looked at Curly.

"Are you ready for a riding adventure?" he asked.

"I think so, but I'm not sure."

He assisted her, and as she settled in the saddle, she realized his teaching expertise was in helping beginners.

"Rosie, right?"

"Yes." She gazed at the beautiful blond curls that reached the collar of his shirt. "And you're Curly?"

"Yes, mam," he said with a dashing smile. "Don't worry, Jack is a friendly horse, but don't let him get close to the other horses. He kicks occasionally."

Rosa was nervous about drawing attention to herself, but Jack behaved, and the ride was uneventful. When Curly helped her dismount, he held on longer than he had to, part of the act. Still, she couldn't ignore the flutter of a feeling she couldn't describe.

That night, Angelica met her new fling and soon forgot Rosa was with her. Rosa tried to be content as she sat alone and listened to the music. The Cowboys were in attendance that night. Wyatt looked at Rosa, then at Curly. "Looks like you're up," he said to Curly.

Curly didn't mind asking Rosa to dance. He was 6'4" and usually had trouble finding a dance partner his size. He guessed Rosa was almost six feet tall. She turned beet red, humiliated as he approached her. She wanted to dance, but knew he felt obligated to ask. Rosa had a background in dance and followed his country swing with ease. He was a fabulous lead. Rosa couldn't help being swept off her feet. He was funny, friendly, and popular; the little kids adored him. She was certain he had better things to do than dance with her, but they stayed on the dance floor, and within a short time it seemed like they had been practicing for years. Curly understood the position Rosa was in; the D'Augellis were too busy drinking and partying to notice her sitting alone. Curly attended the clubhouse every night to dance with her.

On the last night of her stay, Angelica went to dinner with her new boyfriend. Rosa didn't mind being alone, and visited the horses in the pasture before dark. She had become fond of Snowball and brought apple slices as a treat.

"Thank you, Snowball. You are such a good girl," she whispered. "I'll never forget you or this vacation, and I hope you'll always be happy." Snowball nuzzled her, grateful for the attention. Rosa turned when she heard someone walking behind her.

"Hi Rosie"

"Hi Curly"

"You've made a friend there, Rosie; horses can sense when someone likes them. You two have formed a bond."

Rosa tried to think of something to say, since they hadn't talked much at the clubhouse. "How do you like being a cowboy?" she asked.

"It's a summer job, so I can't call myself a cowboy. I don't know if you noticed, but I am not in the rodeo, and they give me beginner classes."

"Well, what do you do?"

"Besides getting in trouble? I'm a student; I just graduated high school and will attend college next year."

Rosa smiled. He was only two years older.

"How about you, Rosie? Is your next gig bull riding?" he asked jokingly.

"No silly. I will be a junior when school starts, but I'm unsure about my college plans. I might like to attend college out of state and major in biology."

"Interesting subject. I am going into business."

There was a long, comfortable silence between them. Curly knew she was leaving in the morning. He wanted to let her know that he had enjoyed the time they had spent dancing together.

"I had a good time on the dance floor, Rosie."

Curly looked at Rosa. He liked her. She was quiet and not chatty like most girls her age. When he danced with her, he was aware of a growing attraction. She had an exotic look about her; in her eyes. He couldn't tell what color they were; they seemed light, sometimes green, sometimes blue. In the fading sunlight, they looked green with a darker blue around her iris and a gold starburst radiating from the center. She was bold enough to hold his gaze. She had a delicate figure, like a dancer. He noticed her lips; they were full and looked soft with just a hint of lip gloss. She was young and sweet; he wanted to hold her and wondered if she had ever been kissed. As he gazed into those mesmerizing eyes, he saw intensity and knew she wanted something from him. He felt an unexpected desire as he put his arms around her. She didn't resist. Rosa felt right in his arms as he kissed her gently. Afterward, when she gave him a grateful smile; he realized he had sent the wrong message. They would probably never see each other again, and he wanted her to remember him. Suddenly he longed for a more passionate kiss. She met him halfway as he leaned into her. There was nothing innocent in this kiss. They responded to the embrace, surprised by the intensity. Rosa relaxed, shocked by the powerful longing she felt in his arms. Finally, she pulled away and looked at him with a sad smile.

"Thank you, Curly. I knew there was a reason I came on this trip."

Curley watched her as she turned and walked to her cabin. He was certain she didn't recognize her power and allure. He tended the horses. The taste of strawberry lip gloss lingered on his lips.

Chapter 1

TEN YEARS LATER

Yale always called her Rose instead of Rosa. She wondered if he wanted to ignore her Cuban heritage. Rosa did not resemble her Cuban mother, except for her unusual eye color, or her father, who was English. She knew Yale and his family were society types who preferred to think of her as having an English background. Yale brought her home to his family for Christmas, and she celebrated the holiday away from her parents for the first time. Rosa's mother was thrilled; she encouraged Rosa to date Yale because he was studying to be a doctor and because his family was wealthy. She reminded Rosa how fortunate she was that Yale had taken an interest in her. She dated him in college; he was a popular guy on campus, and she was thrilled. Her sorority sisters were surprised when he asked her out, and even more astonished when the relationship seemed to last. When Yale entered the university's medical school program, she stayed in the area to attend dental school. They were both devoted to their studies but saw each other often. She prepared meals for him and warmed his bed. She comforted him through the grueling days of medical school but kept the challenges of dental school to herself. He didn't need her problems on top of his own. Graduation was in May, and she was ready for the next step. It seemed logical that he would propose at Christmas, and since she was spending the week with his family, she was certain he would ask.

The Dixon family gatherings were formal, and Rosa tried to adapt. She lacked the social finesse expected of her. When she set the table, she put the forks in the wrong place; she gagged when she tried caviar and prayed she could keep it down. His family seemed stiff and distant, and she wondered if she could fit in. His mother and sister acted reserved, and Mrs. Dixon treated her like the hired help.

"Rose, would you mind getting a piece of cake for Yale?" or, "I think Yale needs another beer."

Despite her expectations, he didn't propose, and the week became stressful and uncomfortable. Her Christmas present was in a jewelry box but was the wrong size for a ring. She had waited six years, and was disappointed, and hurt. When they left the Dixon estate, their conversation was strained. Rosa wondered if their floundering relationship could survive but waited to see what would happen next.

***

A confrontation happened on Valentine's Day, which fell on a Sunday. Yale promised to meet her for 7 pm Mass and dinner at her apartment afterward. When he didn't show up, she left the church alone and returned to her apartment to wait for him. At 10 pm when he finally arrived, she realized she could no longer tolerate his careless disregard for her feelings.

"Thanks a lot, Yale, you could have called."

" I'm sorry, I forgot about the time." He handed her a dozen roses. "Happy Valentine's Day."

She was in no mood to celebrate. "So tell me, Yale, what happens next?"

"What do you mean?"

"I have boards to take before I can get a dental license. Should I take the Midwest board?"

"Well, that's up to you."

"What are you planning to do, Yale?"

"I am looking into residency programs. I'm considering one in California."

"I guess that doesn't include me."

"You're welcome to come with me."

"Newsflash, there's no such thing as a traveling dentist. I need to settle somewhere so I can get established. I can't follow you around the country without a commitment."

He hesitated, then whispered, "I'm not ready."

"I don't think you will ever be ready, Yale. We've dated for six years, enough time to make up your mind. Let's face it, it's not going to happen." She tried to compose herself, but couldn't hold back the tears. She was furious. "The dinner is ruined. Get out."

"Can't we talk about this, Rose?"

" The name is Rosa. Get out." She threw a dozen roses at him as she pushed him out the door and watched him stumble down the stairwell of her apartment. "Don't come back; we're through."

***

In the morning she went to Dean Gallagher's office in the dental school to get advice about her career. She did not want to tell her parents about her breakup with Yale; she was certain her mother would insist she crawl back to him. The dean greeted her with a friendly smile.

"Dr. Fletcher, it's nice to see you. What can I do for you?" The dean was a large man with a warm handshake and a big heart. He had helped other women in her class, who looked to him as a father figure.

"Thank you for seeing me," she started. "There is a change in my circumstances, and I would like advice about my plans. I signed up for the Midwest board exam, but now I think I will move to New Jersey. Perhaps I should take the Northeast regional board instead."

The dean sensed she was on the verge of tears. He wanted her to know she could confide in him. "If you tell me what's wrong, Rosa, I might be better equipped to give you advice."

The heartache was still raw, and she started to cry. He handed her a box of tissues, and he waited.

"I have been going out with my boyfriend for six years; he is in medical school and will soon start a residency program. It seems we are going to go our separate ways."

"Are you sure about this, Rosa?"

"I'm sure. It's over."

"My suggestion is to take both boards. You have already signed up for the Midwest board. It will be practice for the Northeast board even if you do not stay in the Midwest. You will then have a choice if your situation changes."

"I'm sure it won't."

The dean thought about what he should say next. She would take his suggestions seriously, and his comments would influence her moving forward. To her surprise, he took her hand and expressed his heartfelt sympathy. "When I was in dental school, my long-time girlfriend broke up with me. She didn't want to deal with the long study hours, my anxieties, or my moods. I realized that my decision to go into dentistry meant I needed a supportive partner. She wasn't. I know how it feels, Rosa; it hurt so much I thought I would never get over it. When I married years later, I realized my wife was worth the wait; she's the one I belong with. The unexpected turns in our lives often result in happiness different from the one we imagined."

"I appreciate your being candid, Dean Gallagher. I know I'm not the first one to go through this."

"You're allowed to grieve, as it is a loss. But everything happens for a reason. It's not easy to choose a direction in life, but you are young, healthy, and quite beautiful, and you should enjoy your young adulthood and not worry about what happens next." He paused and tried to think of a way he could assist her. "Do you know Rebecca Monahan?"

"Yes, she was my TA in dental materials when I was a sophomore."

"She's living and practicing in northern New Jersey. She would happily help you with boards and anything else you need. Should I reach out to her on your behalf?"

"That would be great, Dean Gallagher. Rebecca is so nice; she would be a helpful contact in New Jersey."

When Rosa returned to her apartment that night, the phone was ringing. Yale tried calling her many times, but she would not answer the phone. She was doing him a favor, as they were destined to move in different directions. There were things she loved about Yale: his passion to be a doctor, the protective way he put his arm around her, the bravado that hid the secret insecurities she knew he had. But he had not loved her back in a way that satisfied her, and he rarely put her feelings before his own. And ultimately, he would not commit.

The reality was heartbreaking, but she realized she was trying too hard to make it work. It wasn't meant to be.

Chapter 2

After the initial shock, Rosa experienced a sense of relief and felt empowered by her newfound freedom. She no longer had to consider Yale's needs; she could decide what to do and where to live. Yale had been her only love interest, except for that young cowboy she met at the ranch. She sometimes wondered what had happened to Curly. Rosa had little experience dating and wondered if men would be interested in her. Her friend Lisa insisted on a girls' night out when she realized Rosa was no longer seeing Yale.

"Have you been to Chuck's place? It's the local night spot that features jazz musicians."

"No, but I always wanted to go."

"I'll take you there on Friday. It's a dental school hangout, and I'm sure you'll have fun. The two bartenders are junior dental students. They are entertaining, and one of them sometimes sings with the band."

Rosa hadn't been out for months, so she spent extra time on her hair and makeup. She forgot how exciting it was to go out with a girlfriend on a Friday night. It was interesting to see her colleagues in a social setting. One classmate described his participation in a professional golf tour. Another was a certified instructor in skydiving. Rosa realized she was part of a fun and exciting group. The bartender had a fabulous voice, and she complimented him when she ordered a drink at the bar.

Rosa thought about missed opportunities in undergraduate and dental school. She didn't attend class parties because Yale did not want to go and he did not want her to go alone. It caused arguments, and she soon realized that he would not impose limitations if he trusted her. She regretted her isolation from social events and wondered what the four years would have been like if she had not devoted so much time to him. She missed out as an undergraduate too, but what choice did she have but to move ahead?

Yale tried to contact her one more time a few days before graduation. He knocked on her apartment door, and she let him in. He pleaded with her. "Rosa, please don't throw away the six years we spent together. I was wrong to leave you out of my plans after graduation. We can still work things out."

"Listen, Yale, I don't want to argue with you, and I don't want to hurt you. The worst thing I could do is coerce you into a marriage you don't want. You deserve a socialite, a girl who will satisfy your family and follow you, always putting your career first. I need a partner who wants to settle in one place so I can establish myself and start a practice. I don't know what we were thinking; our match was unworkable from the start."

"You're mistaken, Rosa. I can make concessions too. I wasn't aware of your situation since you never discussed it with me."

"Exactly my point. You don't think of my career seriously and will always give it a back seat to your own. You're ambitious and would be content with a partner who will follow you wherever the opportunity for advancement might be. I'm sure there is a woman who will adore you and your life choices. I'm sorry, but it won't be me."

He was crying. She hugged him. "Wish me the best and let me go. It's what I want."

***

Rosa's parents flew in for graduation, ready to help her move, but it wasn't the joyous occasion Rosa had imagined. She was heartbroken to see Dr. Yale Dixon accept his degree; the plan had been to move forward as a couple after graduation. Instead, they left each other and everything they had known for the past eight years. Rosa's mother was not happy and wouldn't stop talking about Yale. Rosa became agitated with her relentless nagging.

"You missed your chance, Rosa. You should have put your career on hold and followed him."

"Perhaps I would have considered it if he had placed a ring on my finger. He did me a favor; he's not right for me since he didn't love me enough to commit."

"You should have been more patient and waited until he was ready too."

"I think six years is long enough to wait."

"He is such a great catch; he's worth waiting for."

"Why don't you marry him then?"

"Don't be ridiculous."

***

It was a long and silent ride to New Jersey, and there was a definite chill between Rosa and her mother. The plunge into the unknown was a leap of faith, and Rosa started to lose her nerve. A new life meant leaving all her friends and contacts behind; her only emotional support was from her father. Rosa's inexperienced heart had only known Yale, and she wondered if it was possible to find someone new. She might discover romance but wanted a man to love her with the same intensity that she could love. Was that too much to hope for?

Chapter 3

Alex hopped down the steps on one foot. Russ held his crutches and wondered if this was a good idea. "Are you sure you can travel three blocks in the dark on those crutches?"

"I can't stay in the house any longer; Nana is going to smother me."

The local restaurant was a popular meeting place for young singles, so Alex and Russ took advantage of its proximity to their grandmother's house. They could drink and not worry about driving home. It often saved them from making reckless decisions, since they could not bring girls back to their grandmother's house late at night.

"I'm sure you'll get plenty of sympathy at the bar," noted Russ. "I hope you plan to milk it."

Russ and Alex Montgomery looked like brothers, but were first cousins. Alex was tall, blond-haired, and blue-eyed with a full head of curls, and Russ, taller with curly brown hair and bright blue eyes. They both attracted plenty of female attention, though some women lacked enthusiasm when they told them about their jobs.

"I suppose your injury puts a damper on your female pursuits," joked Russ.

"Stories of my female pursuits are greatly exaggerated. I wish my life were half as exciting as the gossip at the dance studio."

"Should I feel sorry for you, Al? All these beautiful young dancers think of you as a notorious womanizer, while the women who meet me think of me in their basement with rusty pipes."

" Don't start, Russ. You own a business and are saving for a house. I, on the other hand, am still floundering. I have no idea what I am going to do next. Your future is predictable with one component missing. You need a wife. Go out and pick one."

"Life isn't as simple as it was back in Nana's day. Grandpa proposed after two dates. Men and women just found someone they liked and took the plunge; they didn't expect to find a soulmate. Today's women expect more, and don't think about happily ever after with their plumber."

"I'm not taken seriously either, Russ. They tend to dismiss me right away. I have this reputation Fred and Jackie Donovan created for me so there would be no confusion about my being straight. A lasting relationship with a girlfriend is improbable until I get my act together and women change their impression of me."

"Perhaps it is time to reinvent ourselves; we can start tonight. I should concentrate on being more interesting because I have nothing to talk about besides bowling league and plumbing."

They contemplated their situation. Drinking beer made everything seem more promising. Alex limited his intake since he didn't want to re-injure himself on the way home. He was about to make a major life change: to secure a nine-to-five job and change his creative focus from performing to teaching. After high school graduation, he applied to college as a prospective business major but needed a scholarship, so he tried out for a dance scholarship and was offered a full ride. He worked hard and graduated with a double major in business and dance, and accepted a spot in a dance company. He enjoyed dancing and traveling with the company but knew this lifestyle was short term, and his injury forced him to change his plans. When he returned to his hometown, he found a job in accounting and planned to teach classes at Donovan Dance Studio to keep his dance career active. His recent move back had more to do with his Nana than changing career plans and his injury. She was getting older and needed financial help.

"So, is Nana giving you a hard time?" asked Russ.

"Isn't that a woman's job?" he asked sarcastically.

"Nana is no ordinary woman, Alex."

"She is spoiling me, Russ. She makes my bed and does my laundry, and I have gained five pounds. I go to Sunday Mass with her and have even gone to confession. She is determined to make me a fine, respectable young man."

"It sounds like she's prepping you to join the seminary."

Alex smiled. "I'm sure the seminary wouldn't want me. I have broken too many rules."

"I'll come over," Russ offered, "so she can give me some of that attention. I would enjoy a home-cooked meal."

***

The patrons in the bar were in a festive mood since it was the first weekend in June and the weather had turned to summer. Russ helped Alex hobble back to their grandmother's house. She was asleep, but Alex's bedsheets were turned down with a pair of pajamas waiting for him. Nana made up the couch for Russ with two feather pillows, a fluffy quilt, and a similar pair of pajamas. The pants were too short for her two tall boys. They tiptoed around since Buster, her pet parakeet, was in the kitchen with a blanket over his cage. They didn't want to disturb him. The lazy summer days pressed forward, with Russ providing camaraderie and support to his cousin while Alex re-acclimated to life back in his hometown.

Chapter 4

Rosa arranged a meeting with Rebecca Monahan soon after she returned to New Jersey. Rebecca was an associate dentist in the office of Dr. Sabarini, a dentist in his 70s who was semi-retired. After suffering a heart attack, his cardiologist told him to cut his hours. Dr. Sabarini hired Rebecca to help him meet the clinical demands of his busy office. Dr. Sabarini was just getting used to the concept of women in dentistry. He realized there would be many more women dentists in the future and was in awe of the two lovely women standing before him. Rosa was a tall, attractive blond with dramatic coloring, and Rebecca was also tall, with red hair and green eyes. He smiled at both women and wished he were forty years younger.

"Feel free to use the office to screen patients for boards," he offered to Rosa. "If you need additional patients, I'm sure I can help."

"Thank you, Dr. Sabarini. This is so convenient; the dental school is a few miles away."

After he left for the day, Rebecca showed Rosa around the office. Rebecca seemed satisfied with her job. "Dr. Sabarini has been a wonderful mentor. He did not intend to hire a female dentist, but I was available and he needed help immediately. The association seemed unlikely at first, but somehow it works."

"Is he planning to retire?"

"Maybe eventually, but he is still very active, and I assume he would be unhappy if he didn't have this office."

Rebecca was there to help Rosa pass her dental boards. She gave her helpful advice. "I hope you can pass; even though I failed the board at first, I recovered quickly, and it only set me back a couple of months. Do not allow anxiety to consume you. I did not finish the first time because the casting on my gold inlay distorted and would not seat intra-orally. I suggest you schedule a gold foil procedure instead."

Rosa hesitated. "I never did a gold foil."

Rebecca asked, "How many gold inlays did you do in dental school?"

"Two."

"It's ridiculous that these requirements are still on the dental boards; gold is too expensive. Believe me; the gold foil is a more predictable procedure. You can practice on extracted teeth."

Rosa noticed jars of extracted teeth in Dr. Sabarini's lab. Rebecca smiled and warned, "You can't use any of those."

"Why not?"

"The jars contain unusual teeth extracted by Dr. Sabarini. Some have four or five roots. He likes to show them to his colleagues."

Rosa examined the jars and thought about how weird it was to be a dentist. "I don't enjoy extractions."

" Neither do I. Dr. Sabarini and I make a good team because we complement each other. He is not interested in performing cosmetic procedures, like veneers, and I would rather not do surgeries."

Rosa found board patients by screening her family. Her mother was her periodontal patient, Grandpa Diaz was her denture patient, and her Uncle Eddie was there for a gold foil. The school giving the test was unfamiliar, but with Rebecca's help, Rosa passed the exam and applied for her New Jersey state dental license.

When Rosa interviewed for jobs, she discovered her opportunities were limited. She would have preferred a residency program, but students who had studied in New Jersey already filled those positions. Most private offices would only interview dentists with two years of experience or who had completed a residency. After many interviews, she accepted a job at Dental Connections, a busy insurance office. They were looking for a female dentist and hired her. The owner, Dr. Schwartz, worked on patients part-time and oversaw business operations. The office was open six days a week and had three associate dentists, one hygienist, and a full-time office manager and support staff. Rosa was part-time, working three days. When Rosa approached her first patient, the woman burst into tears. "What happened to the other doctor?" she sobbed.

Rosa did her best to calm the patient. "Dr. Richards is no longer working here; I don't know the details. Would you like to speak to the office manager?"

"How is that going to help? "she lamented. "Today we were supposed to discuss a treatment plan."

"Dr. Richards left detailed notes," Rosa replied. "Let's go over them together and see what we can come up with."

Rosa gradually gained the woman's trust, and they agreed to move forward with the plan already approved by the insurance. The patient was most concerned with her appearance, and when Rosa suggested they start with fillings in the front, the patient rescheduled with her. Rosa later learned that Dr. Schwartz had assigned the patient to her to see how she would handle the situation. He knew she would be an asset to the practice because of her patience and professionalism. Rosa partnered with an experienced dental assistant, who would make her introduction to private practice less stressful. Dawn, her assistant, was certified, and the patients loved her offbeat sense of humor and her ability to make them feel at ease. She was young, and fun, and Rosa looked forward to working with her.

The commute from her parents' house was long, and sometimes she confronted heavy traffic. Rosa looked for housing near her new job. Dental Connections was close to Donovan's Dance Studio, where she took lessons as a child. She was happy to see Donovan Dance still in business, and she signed up for adult classes in ballet and jazz, hoping to meet women her age also interested in dance.

Chapter 5

The days at Dental Connections were crazy and busy; Rosa was happy she had not taken on full-time hours at that office. She needed a second job but wanted a change of pace. She scheduled an interview at a county-run nursing home, an environment much different from private practice. Rosa viewed the opportunity as exciting and rewarding. She imagined the residents had dental needs that were not being addressed.

The large stone building was old but impressive. As Rosa entered the large foyer, she signed in with a security guard, who directed her to the dental clinic. After passing several administrative offices, she found it. The clinic was spacious, with cabinets that lined the back wall, a single dental chair and X-ray unit, and a desk occupied by a pleasant older woman who greeted her with a warm smile.

"Hello, I'm Dottie. You must be Dr. Fletcher."

"Nice to meet you, Dottie. Are you going to interview me today?"

"Oh, no, Dr. Ryan will be here shortly, but you can ask me questions, and I will do my best to answer them."

"Thank you. What is your role at the clinic?"

"I'm a dental assistant. I trained for this position in a senior citizen program and work 20 hours per week. It is a start-up project, and the whole concept is new. Besides assisting, I will be in charge of scheduling patients and the paperwork needed for Medicaid submission."

Rosa looked around the room. Large windows lined the side wall, and the atmosphere was pleasant. The room was too big for a single operatory, but they might foresee expansion in the future. The equipment was familiar to Rosa. She imagined a partition would be necessary to separate the treatment area from the rest of the room. "Is Dr. Ryan a dentist?" asked Rosa.

"No, Dr. Ryan is the attending physician. Providing dental care for the residents has been a priority since he started here last year, and finally, he secured the funding to accomplish it. It has been difficult to transport patients to a dentist, and most dental problems were addressed only when the patient presented with an emergency."

Just then, Dr. Ryan walked in; he was young and attractive with a gorgeous smile; not what she expected. He caught her off guard. She waited quietly as he approached. "Dr. Fletcher, pleased to meet you. I'm Gerry Ryan. Welcome to the clinic."

Rosa handed him her resume and smiled. "I didn't expect the facility to be so well equipped. I'm impressed."

Dr. Ryan had a soft, calm way about him; he put Rosa at ease. He was also to the point and discussed the situation. "The response to my ad has been disappointing. The proposed schedule works for the facility, but hiring a dentist for two half days has been challenging."

She responded to the comment with enthusiasm. "I am available for your hours, since I have struggled to coordinate with my current part-time position."

"And where are you working now?"

"At Dental Connections, a short drive from here. They know I plan to find an additional job and will give me a reference."

He studied her resume. "I see you are a recent graduate. If hired, you would be the only dentist. Are you comfortable working alone?"

"I am. I prefer not to do difficult extractions, but I could refer extensive procedures to a surgeon at the hospital. I have experience in geriatric dentistry. This might be a good fit for me."

He hesitated and tried to be forthcoming with his next comment. "Your pay would be through Medicaid reimbursement. We do not have staff experienced in handling the claims; the business office would be happy to assist, but I doubt they are qualified. Dental and medical claims are not comparable. You would submit the claims yourself with Dottie's help."

"I will have to figure out how to deal with insurance if ever I have my own office. It could be a learning experience. Since the hospital covers the cost of my assistant and materials, the compensation should be satisfactory."

Dr. Ryan once again viewed her resume. "I am interested, Dr. Fletcher. I will check your references and let you know."

Rosa had a good feeling about the interview. Dr. Ryan was dreamy, like those doctors on TV. She doubted she would see him if she took the job; he would be too busy to visit the dental clinic. Still, she felt a spark of interest when she met him.

Donovan Dance Studio was only two miles from the geriatric hospital. She had time to eat a light dinner and to arrive in time for the class. Ten women enrolled in the ballet class; all young and serious about dance. The course listed itself as a beginner class, but Rosa noticed the other students had broken in their ballet slippers. They were not beginners. Jackie Donovan was teaching the class, and when she read off the class roster, she remembered Rosa as a little girl.

"Hello Sarah Bernhardt," she said with a smile, and Rosa replied, " Hi, Miss Jackie." She looked at her dance teacher. "I never understood why you called me Sarah Bernhardt."

Jackie laughed. "She was a silent movie star, popular way before your time. You reminded me of her; you were so dramatic as a little girl."

"I was?"

"Yes, and I do not believe people change that much. You have an inner Sarah Bernhardt, Rosa."

"But I am so shy. I'm sure no one would describe me as dramatic."

"You will show your true self to someone. Perhaps it will manifest itself in dance. That is what I expected of you, but your family moved before you could develop it."

Rosa enjoyed seeing Miss Jackie, and the students were there to work. Miss Jackie was just as strict with her adult students as she was with the children. Her methods had produced many talented dancers; some had continued to become professional dancers.

During the break, the ballet students remained, and more women joined them. They talked about the new instructor teaching the jazz class. He was a professional dancer taking a sabbatical from touring because of an injury. He was also known as a notorious womanizer.

Alex was waiting in the business office and overheard their comments. He was self-conscious about the rumors, though he had perpetuated the impression with some of his rakish remarks and antics. He assumed a more serious persona with this class and conducted it with professional aloofness. There was a hush in the room when he entered the studio. He was tall. He was handsome. He had the physique of a well-toned athlete. Rosa couldn't believe it. Her dance instructor was Curly from the ranch. She tried to hide herself in the back, but being 5'11", she couldn't blend in. As he scanned the room, he gave her a second look, but he didn't recognize her. Rosa was certain he did not remember her. He stood before the class, played Led Zeppelin's H*ouses of the Holy,* an unusual choice, and started isolations. Alex was all business and acted like he was teaching because he had to. At the conclusion, a cooldown and a simple statement. "Thank you, ladies. I'll see you next week."

As Rosa was leaving, he glanced at her again with no glimmer of recognition. The attitude of the students had changed.

"He's gorgeous, but a little scary."

"I think he's upset because he's injured and has to subject himself to a group of hopeless beginners. I'm sure he would prefer to be on tour."

"We did look bad. Only the ballet students were able to keep up."

Rosa kept her thoughts to herself. That wasn't the guy she knew from the ranch. It was the most strenuous dance class she had ever taken. Alex had been a professional dancer for years and had unrealistic expectations of what he could accomplish with a beginner class. Rosa drove an hour back to her parents' house, then took a long soak in a hot tub to soothe her aching muscles.

Back at the dance school, Alex hid in the business office. He did not want to socialize with the students since he planned to remain distant and reserved. Miss Jackie joined him after the students left. "Alex, what's the matter with you? I never knew you could be such a hardass. You are normally so charming when with a group of women."

"It is intimidating to have twenty attractive women watching my every move for over an hour."

"Since when? I'm surprised at you, Al. You always seem so comfortable around women." Then she looked at him curiously. "That tall blond seems to be just your type."

"Forget it, Jackie. She's the one who seemed determined to hide herself from me, though it was hard not to notice her. She is very graceful for someone so tall."

"Just like someone else I know."

"Listen, Jackie, I will be better prepared next week. I hope I didn't scare any of them off. Did any students drop out?"

"No, just the opposite. They asked if there was more room in the class for their friends. I had to tell them we could not take additional students."

"I do have an idea for the class. They seem so graceful and feminine, especially your ballet students. I will choreograph a jazz routine that will showcase their assets. It will be exciting to add new steps each week."

"That's a great idea, Alex. You don't have to alter your teaching methods because they are adults. After all, we are children at heart."

Chapter 6

Alex grew up in the large, two-family brick house built by his grandfather. A common hallway on the first floor led to his grandmother's apartment and the tenants upstairs. The occupants shared the laundry room and den in the basement. Alex had fond memories of the house, and the tenants who lived upstairs had always been like family. The decor had not changed in years; Nana was religious, and the house looked like a shrine. Statues of the Virgin Mary and samplers with Bible verses decorated the space, as well as doilies and knick-knacks. He loved Nana and his home, but was often relieved to escape to the simplicity of his room, which contained a queen bed, a dresser, and a stereo. The walls were bare. He liked to keep things simple. He visited the house often, but had never intended to move back. His grandfather had been gone for twenty years, and Nana had been self-sufficient. Now she needed his help, and his injury was a likely excuse for his return.

"Did you have fun prancing about?" she asked when he walked through the door.

"Sure, Nana. I love to dance, but I don't enjoy the scrutiny of so many women watching my every move."

"I have seen the pretty girls at the dance studio. Don't you think it is time to be less flippant? Maybe have a girlfriend?"

"It's not that simple, Nana. Don't worry. I like girls. So does Russ. It's complicated."

"My friend, Mrs. Sidorski, has a nice granddaughter."

"Thanks, Nana, but I enjoy being a bachelor. Russ would like to have a steady girlfriend."

"Russell has no self-confidence, but I don't know why. He's a handsome lad, though he can be a bit goofy."

Alex was shocked Nana said that out loud. He tried to reassure her. "Just give him time; Russ is an acquired taste; he has to find the right girl."

"Or she needs to find him. He's clueless, Alex. Can't you do anything to help him?"

"I'll try, but I haven't had much luck myself."

Buster was flitting about in his cage, excited that Alex was home. It was nine o'clock, and Nana was ready to call it a night. Buster and Alex had a routine: a late-night snack and music before bed. "How about Steely Dan tonight?" he asked, and Buster cocked his head as though he understood. Alex started the album, gave Buster an orange crunch stick, and poured himself a beer. Alex enjoyed talking to Buster, and the bird relaxed at the sound of his voice. "I need a change, Bud, but I don't know what to do next. Nana thinks I should have a girlfriend, but I'm not a promising prospect for a woman who wants a long-term relationship. I don't have much to offer. What do you think?"

The question upset Buster, and he cackled; too much excitement. Alex turned the music off and placed the blanket over his cage. The parakeet calmed down. Alex went to bed too; he had to be at the accounting office by 8 am.

Rosa took the job at the nursing home and was anxious to start. She could walk from one job to another and realized how easy her life would be if she lived nearby. She saw an ad in the local newspaper for a room to rent and called. A young woman answered the phone.

"Hello"

"Hi, I saw your ad in the paper. My name is Rosa Fletcher, and I am looking for a place to live close to work."

"Hi Rosa, I'm Connie. My roommates and I share a four-bedroom house, and we are looking for another roommate. The location is in a safe residential community, and the rent is $175 plus utilities. We are in our 20s and are looking for someone career-oriented and friendly. Are you interested?"

"I am. The location is convenient for work, and I would like to make new friends since I have been out of state for many years."

"What do you do, Rosa?"

"I'm a dentist."

"Oh, how exciting! Can you come by tomorrow night? Mary Lou and Chrissy will be home, and we can get acquainted."

"Perfect. What time?"

"Does 7 o'clock work?"

***

Rosa drove to the house, hopeful. The neighborhood was nice; roomy four-bedroom colonials stood on small lots. She parked on the street and walked up several steps, past two white lion statues. The decor looked Italian. When Connie answered the door, Rosa entered a two-story foyer with an ornate chandelier that illuminated the hallway. The walls were busy with black and white wallpaper, and pristine black-and-white tiles on the floor. She noted a red wall-to-wall carpet beyond. Connie gave Rosa a knowing glance. "We didn't decorate the house; I personally prefer more subdued tones. The red carpet is hard to match. Come into the kitchen to meet Mary Lou and Chrissy."

The girls smiled when they met Rosa. They looked about the same age. Connie did most of the talking and asked some roommate-appropriate questions. She was a cute redhead with freckles and a friendly smile. Mary Lou had a Southern accent and was petite with wavy brown hair. She seemed outspoken. Chrissy did modeling in New York. She was younger than the other girls, but independent and sure of herself. Rosa imagined Chrissy had men calling her all the time; she was stunning. After the meeting in the kitchen, Chrissy took Rosa on a tour of the house, which looked comfy, and was furnished with style. The family room had a faint scent of cinnamon. They climbed the steps to the bedroom for rent; a corner room with one window facing the driveway and another overlooking the backyard. It was spacious and unfurnished, and Rosa wondered what she had to match the red carpet. Chrissy was the most recent addition to the household.

"I have been here for five months, Rosa. It is a nice place to live, but Connie and Mary Lou have steady boyfriends who stay here on the weekends. I wanted you to know, just in case that is an issue. I wish I had a roommate who was unattached and interested in going out to clubs." She gave Rosa a hopeful look.

"I love to dance, Chrissy, and no, I don't have a boyfriend. I don't know many people in the area, and hope to have a social life."

"Would you like to take the room?"

"Yes, I would."

Chrissy smiled; she was radiant. "You can have the room as soon as you're ready. On Sunday, Charlie and Louis will be here if you need help. Charlie is a contractor who has dated Connie for a few years, and

Louis is Mary Lou's boyfriend. I know they would move and assemble furniture if necessary."

"Thanks, Chrissy. I'm eager to be your new roommate. I'll be here on Sunday afternoon."

***

Rosa's parents were disappointed she was moving, but realized their daughter had been away at school for years and assumed her stay with them would be short. She packed her bedroom furniture into a small U-Haul and moved on Sunday. Charlie helped her assemble her bed and hung the white curtains her mother had given her. She was relieved the curtains were the right size for the windows since she hadn't thought to measure. The patchwork quilt did not clash with the red carpet, and she was pleased. As she organized her toiletries on a shelf in the upstairs bathroom, she realized this was the most absurd room in the house. The striped wallpaper was on all four walls and the door, leaving the impression there was no exit. Her pink towels did not match the lime green and lemon yellow stripes, but she didn't think that was an issue. The guest bathroom was downstairs. Only the girls would use the hideous one upstairs. As Rosa settled into her new room, she felt content. She had accomplished so much in a few months and had made a life for herself. Rosa would try to enjoy her social life without worrying about what would happen next.

The work week was busy for Rosa because of her second job, and she was becoming well-versed in the paperwork required to submit Medicaid claims. Dottie was a professional assistant and a hard worker; attentive and kind to the residents. The dental clinic was Dr. Ryan's pet project, and he stopped by to see how Rosa was doing. Dr. Ryan was popular with the nurses and the administrative staff, who always raved about him. Rosa intended to remain professional, though she wanted to flirt. Rosa was a doctor and thought it inappropriate to cross that boundary.

***

On Saturday night, Rosa went out with Chrissy. She wore her favorite white cotton jumpsuit to show off her slim figure. Chrissy wore a tight-fitting leopard print jumpsuit that would attract the attention of every man at the bar. Chrissy led the way into the disco, and the experience was like the parting of the Red Sea. Her beauty and self-confidence were on display, and Rosa was in awe of how this twenty-two-year-old was so sure of herself. Rosa enjoyed dancing, and when she was on the dance floor with Chrissy, men stood nearby to cut in. This was new to Rosa, who felt like she was learning the art of meeting men from an expert. The girls discussed their night out as they drove home.

"I had a great time, Chrissy. I can't believe how effortless it was for you to meet new people. I had a steady boyfriend for six years and have never been confident enough to venture beyond my group of friends."

"You are shy, Rosa, but if there is a guy you want to talk to, you should not hesitate. Any man will be flattered, even if he is not interested in dating. If he is with friends, he can brag that the pretty blond thought he was interesting."

"It is not in my nature to do something like that. What if he has a girlfriend, or if he's weird in some way and I can't get rid of him?"

"That's why you agree to a talk, or maybe to dance. Don't let him buy you a drink unless you're sure you would like to spend some time with him."

"I can't do that."

"Well, you might as well cross any shy man off your list because they have the same insecurities that you have."

"I guess you're right, Chrissy."

Rosa was thinking more about Dr. Ryan. If the opportunity presented itself, she could be bold and let him know she was interested.

Chapter 7

Ballet was difficult because of the strength and control needed at the barre and on the floor. But Rosa's jazz class was as difficult as any ballet class. Alex Montgomery was unconventional; he started with isolations, usually to a rock group, then worked the floor with jazz, traditional Broadway, or Latin rhythms. At the end of class, he taught them choreography to *Dedicated to the One I Love,* a surprising and intriguing song choice. The vibe fit the class, and Rosa realized Alex was a skilled choreographer who could evaluate the talent and personality of his students. She looked forward to the steps they added to the dance every week. Because she stretched and practiced at home, the classes became easier. Learning from Alex was a rare opportunity, and she savored the chance to look at him since he had become shockingly handsome as a grown man. She remembered how she had dreamed of being his girlfriend years earlier. Now she had fleeting thoughts of being his lover. Alex did not recognize her, but that was not surprising since she had changed. At sixteen, she was a skinny, awkward girl with a boyish figure, brown hair, and braces. When the braces came off, her classmates remarked that her new smile reminded them of the actress doing commercials with the famous New York Jets quarterback, Joe Namath. Rosa saw the commercials and realized she should copy the woman's hairstyle, which was shoulder length and layered with heavy highlights. Rosa wore makeup and had her eyebrows done professionally. The biggest change was in her weight. It changed her look from a girl to a woman and even softened the angular appearance of her face. When Rosa viewed her picture as a freshman in high school, she had to admit the change was drastic. Rosa was sure Yale would not have given her a second thought if she had not improved her looks. She still felt like the mousy young girl who grew up in the summer of 1972. Miss Jackie compared her to Sarah Bernhardt, but she was certain she could never be dramatic. Rosa tried to avoid thoughts of being with Alex since she liked Gerry Ryan, and he was more suitable. But Alex was nice to look at.

***

Rosa visited her parents for the first time since her move. She loved the fall weather, and her childhood home was on a lake. The countryside was bursting with color as she approached their home. The water reflected splashes of autumn on the tree-lined shoreline, and she reveled in the crisp autumn air. It felt like a vacation here in the country, and she missed the lake's changing beauty.

As she hugged her parents, she could feel the stress in her father's arms and realized he did not look well. The strain of his work took a toll on his health. Rosa's grandfather on her mother's side was his partner, and he had become forgetful and unreliable. In desperation, Mr. Fletcher hired a young businessman certified to prepare taxes. The employee was helpful, but he was not a CPA, and Oliver Fletcher bore the burden of the business. He also had to deal with her mother, Anita, who was as lively and troublesome as ever. Anita had not forgiven Rosa for her foolish decision to break up with Yale, but seemed to accept it. Rosa cleared out the remaining items in her closet, a subtle way of telling her mother she had moved beyond her childhood home.

The Fletchers had an unusual family dynamic, and Rosa marveled at how different her parents were. She wondered how they stayed together. Her father kept his feelings to himself. Her mother was outspoken and did not hold back. In the years before Rosa was born, Grandpa Diaz, her mother's father, had joined with Grandpa Fletcher, her father's father, to partner in an accounting firm. When Grandpa Fletcher's son Oliver graduated college and became a CPA, he joined the firm as a young man. They all became a family when Oliver and Anita married and had Rosa. The firm was less productive after Grandpa Fletcher passed away, and now her other grandfather was becoming less reliable. Rosa remembered her Cuban grandmother as being colorful and fun, but she died when Rosa was a small child.

Rosa stayed for dinner and tried to be upbeat. She told her parents they should not worry about her; she was happy working and was having fun with her new roommates. They discussed Thanksgiving, which would only include their immediate family and Grandpa Diaz. Anita relished the days when they had a full table with many guests, and Rosa knew how disappointed her mother was that a married daughter and a son-in-law would not be possible anytime soon.

Chapter 8

Rebecca met Rosa at the local American Dental Association meeting. Rosa was the second woman to join the group. Most members were men who had practiced dentistry for many years, but Rebecca's friend Patrick was also a recent graduate, and he joined both women at the monthly meetings. They had in-depth discussions while dining together, and Rosa enjoyed Patrick's funny observations and looked forward to meeting both of her colleagues.

Rosa also formed a friendship with Dottie, her assistant at the geriatric hospital. The older woman took Rosa under her wing, and their relationship was more personal than professional. The dental clinic became a social setting for the ambulatory patients. Since the clinic was on the main floor, the residents liked to visit. It was the closest they could get to the world outside. Rosa informed Dr. Ryan she needed a barrier between the front desk and the dental chair; she did not mind when the residents stopped by but insisted on privacy during dental procedures. Dr. Ryan provided a curtain much like what you would expect in a hospital room. Rosa performed oral cancer screening on all patients, even ones without teeth. Many had dentures, or were getting by with no teeth or dentures. Rosa could not imagine how they could function, but did not promote dentures to patients who didn't want them. The nurses sometimes sent dentures to Dottie, asking if Dr. Fletcher knew who they belonged to. There was no way she could tell if she had not made it herself. She inscribed the patient's name on the acrylic dentures that she fabricated; that way, if lost, the dentures would be returned.

Dr. Ryan visited the dental clinic often, and Rosa sometimes daydreamed about him. They had developed a comfortable professional relationship, and the admiration seemed mutual. All the single nurses speculated about whom he was going to ask out. He was kind, composed, and soft-spoken. Rosa felt drawn to him and wished she could be the one.

Chapter 9

The leaves fell, the time changed, and Thanksgiving was fast approaching. Rosa was not hiding in the back row of the jazz class; she danced in the front at the extreme corner of the room. She had ample space to dance since the other students avoided this location. A classmate told Rosa she liked to follow Alex while standing behind him, but from Rosa's perspective, she had to follow in the mirror. Rosa suspected her tendency to use the mirror had something to do with dentistry and the ability to use an indirect visual path. Every day when she worked on maxillary teeth, she did so with the help of an intraoral mirror. She found it interesting that she would employ this talent in dance class without realizing it. The dancers improved and had fun, and as they neared the end of their choreographed dance, they noticed a smile on their instructor's face. Alex tried to act aloof and stern but could not perpetuate the pretense. He was proud of the improvements made by his students, and Rosa began seeing Curly instead of the strict and disinterested professional performer he at first seemed to be.

Alex was busy with work at the accounting office, teaching the jazz class, and practicing for a charity performance he had agreed to do. It was a treat to have Thanksgiving weekend off with no particular plans. Nana hosted Thanksgiving and invited his Aunt Mary and the upstairs tenants, Tammy and Lawrence. Tammy was an attractive African-American woman in her 30s who had moved upstairs after the birth of her son eight years earlier. Since she was a single mom who worked, Lawrence spent many after-school hours with Nana, who was home during the day. Lawrence loved to visit Alex and Russ. He needed a male role model, and Alex and Russ did their best to fill the void left by his father, who was out of the picture. They had to temper their conversations since Lawrence was a sponge that absorbed everything they said. After they played games with him, Lawrence settled down and became pensive. He opened up about a heartache he wanted to conceal from his mother. Lawrence had a look far too solemn for an eight-year-old.

"The kids at school want to know why I don't have a dad. I don't know what to say, so I get mad and try not to cry."

After a pause, Alex gave a heartfelt response. "Sometimes that's just the way it is, Lawrence. I didn't have a dad, but had my Grandpa. When he died, Mr. Donovan acted like a father. You can have a family of people who aren't related."

"Like us?"

"Of course. Russ and I will always be here when you need another guy to talk to."

"Are you and Russ coming to the Christmas play?"

"We wouldn't miss it."

They enjoyed a delicious Thanksgiving dinner. Then Tammy, Nana, and Aunt Mary stayed downstairs to clean up and package the leftovers. The basement had a kitchen, a bathroom, and a large meeting area with a long table appropriate for holiday gatherings.

The boys went up the stairs to Nana's apartment because Nana had shooed them out of the basement kitchen. Nana had a special treat for the parakeet and asked Lawrence to place it in Buster's cage. Alex felt sorry for the little bird, who constantly sought attention and seemed lonely, but they were all lonely. Lawrence missed having a dad, Russ longed for female companionship, and so did Alex. To distract Lawrence from his melancholy, Russ talked about desserts; soon Lawrence headed downstairs to make sure his mom claimed the dessert leftovers.

"Be careful on the stairs, Lawrence," warned Alex. The basement was a great place to gather, but the steps were treacherous. Russ said they weren't up to code. He hated it when Lawrence, Nana, or Aunt Mary used the steps. And then the accident they hoped would never happen finally happened. Nana was carrying a dish up the steps, and she tripped. Nana couldn't get up, so they called an ambulance. Alex accompanied her in the vehicle, and Russ followed. Nana had broken a hip, and the physician on call scheduled her for surgery. Alex was going to spend his weekend in the hospital to make arrangements for Nana to have surgery and go to rehab. Nana was resilient and even cheerful, but she had a long road to recovery and many weeks of rehabilitation at a local nursing home. Alex prayed he could care for this wonderful woman who had raised him.

***

Rosa was at the lake during Thanksgiving weekend. She enjoyed staying in her old room but had a restless night; too much turkey and too many desserts. After a few hours of troubled sleep, she woke up in the middle of the night. She had a dream and struggled to recall the details. Her body felt flushed, and she knew the dream had been erotic. The memory was vivid and exciting; a man was encouraging her to relax and enjoy the intimacy. Her dream lover was not Dr. Ryan or Yale. It was Alex.

Chapter 10

When the phone rang in Rosa's room, she thought it might be a work-related call. She heard her mother's voice and thought of her dad since she was worried about his health.

"Is anything wrong, Mom?"

"Your father and I are fine, Rosa. Do you have plans for tomorrow night?"

"No, I will be home after work."

" Would you like to see the Nutcracker? Your father has free tickets and doesn't want to go."

"Sounds like fun. What time?"

"8 pm. I will meet you at the theatre in Morristown. I'm not sure how good it will be; it is a charity event."

"I haven't seen the Nutcracker since I was a little girl. I would love to see it again; I won't set my expectations too high."

It had been years since her father had received complimentary tickets to a holiday show. When Rosa was in grade school, he took her to Radio City Music Hall. Rosa grew up with the dream of becoming a Rockette. In high school, she realized she was too tall to be a professional dancer; even the Rockettes had a height restriction that disqualified her. She gave up the thought of performing and continued to dance just for her enjoyment.

The performing arts theatre was crowded. Rosa was late, but she met her mother, and they hurried to their seats just before the orchestra started. Rosa could not see empty seats, and it appeared that the performance had sold out. She glanced at the program; it read, "Nutcracker Ballet, A Comedy." This was an odd twist. The choreographer designed the performance to be funny. Clara was the only traditional character on stage. The other dancers were strangely cast, and prone to amusing mistakes. Rosa recognized the Mouse King as soon as he appeared on stage. Although he had a mascot-like headpiece on, there was no mistaking the dancer who towered over the others. The bulky headpiece concealed his identity, but Rosa had become familiar with his physique and movements and was impressed that he could dance with that big mouse head blocking his vision. There was a ridiculous scene when the Nutcracker slew the Mouse King, which was hilarious even though it was supposed to be dramatic. The kids in the audience cheered, and the outrageous performance left the crowd in stitches before the intermission.

Rosa looked at the program to confirm the Mouse King was Alex. "Mom, that Mouse King is my jazz teacher."

"Really? Well, no wonder there are so many young ladies in your class."

Rosa thought it was an odd remark from her mother considering that you couldn't see his face. When the house lights dimmed after intermission, the curtain opened after a dramatic pause, and the crowd waited expectantly. The tinkling, crystalline sound of the Sugarplum Fairy was the opening to Act II. When she finally appeared, the audience responded with cheers and riotous laughter. The fairy was 6'4" with blond curls and a dazzling smile. Rosa gasped; it was Alex. He was seriously comical in his white gym shorts, socks, and pink tutu. He performed a difficult dance, and the athleticism shown in his leaps and turns was magnificent. He was by far the most talented Sugarplum Fairy she had ever seen. Rosa looked over at her mother, who could not contain her big smile. She had also seen many performances, but this one was truly unique. The ballet ended with an enthusiastic standing ovation. She was impressed with Alex, as only a very confident man would agree to a performance like that. He had also put time and effort into a project done solely for charity. At jazz class the following week, she couldn't stop smiling. He noticed and smiled back. Her heart did a little flip; it was amazing he still had that effect on her. She was older and wiser now, a professional woman who realized he would not be a good boyfriend. Still, she could not deny the magnetic pull she felt whenever he was around.

***

The four roommates planned a holiday party before Christmas. Rosa bought a bottle of champagne for her roommates; there would be no romance for her this Christmas, but she hoped the other girls would spend time with their boyfriends and enjoy the champagne. Chrissy had a new boyfriend. Rosa didn't know what a Chippendale dancer was, but when she found out she was wary of Chrissy's judgment. Any man who danced for groups of women on stage might engage in flirtations with the women, and possibly more intimate interactions. He must be very handsome, but not a trustworthy boyfriend. She didn't understand Chrissy, as she could have any man she wanted; why him? Rosa would never set herself up for heartbreak like that.

Rosa had holiday parties to attend. Dr. Schwartz rented out the pizzeria next to Dental Connections for a party since it was convenient and more fun than going to a fancy restaurant. The associate dentists and staff were all in attendance, and they had a great time playing silly games and exchanging Secret Santa gifts. Dr. Schwartz was Jewish, so it was nice for him to have a Christmas party and participate in the activities.

***

Dottie and Rosa decorated a small tree and had a party in the dental clinic. They wrapped presents for the residents who stopped by that day. The gifts were items they could use, like playing cards or hand lotion, and extra presents were for any resident who would enjoy them. Dr. Ryan stopped in that afternoon.

"Merry Christmas, Dr. Fletcher, Dottie. I realize this is a spur of the moment, and it is the night before Christmas Eve, but I am taking my administrative staff out tonight and want to invite you to join us." Rosa held her breath. She wanted to go, but not without her assistant.

"I would love to go," replied Dottie. "What time?"

"We are meeting at eight at Mother's Pub."

They both looked at Rosa. "I'm in too, thank you, Dr. Ryan."

Rosa realized she should not read too much into the invitation. The three young women on Dr. Ryan's staff vied for his attention. Inviting Dottie and Rosa might make the evening less awkward for Dr. Ryan, and having additional guests might compel the young women to behave more appropriately. The restaurant was a popular place that Rosa wanted to try, and she looked forward to having dinner with

Dottie. She hoped it would be an opportunity to get to know Dr. Ryan.

Chapter 11

Rosa hoped to make an impression on Dr. Ryan at dinner and wondered if her black dress was too sexy for the occasion. The dress was form-fitting and short, cut low in the back, and showcased her sensuous shape and long legs. She tried it on and accessorized it with dangling earrings that looked like Christmas presents and a holiday pin; the outfit then looked festive and more appropriate. Mother's Pub was a turn-of-the-century brick building on a busy main street, near a residential neighborhood. Soft lighting and rustic decor conveyed a casual and classy ambiance. The restaurant was private, but the adjoining pub was loud and crowded. The aroma in the dining area made one's mouth water. Blackened prime rib and steak were the specials, so Rosa ordered the steak with a salad. Rosa spent most of the evening talking to Dottie. The behavior of Dr. Ryan's staff embarrassed her, as they were loud, drank too much, and ordered the most expensive items on the menu. Dr. Ryan could afford it, but she could see his growing concern about their drinking. Dottie was the adult in the room and told the women they should switch to coffee. Rosa did not have the chance to flirt with Dr. Ryan, and she resigned herself to never having the chance. After dinner, she took a quick look at the pub and then planned to drive home. On her way out, she noticed Patrick sitting at the bar and walked over to wish him a Merry Christmas.

"Hi Pat, fancy meeting you here."

"Merry Christmas, Rosa. What brings you to the neighborhood?"

" I had dinner with my coworkers at the nursing home. How about you?"

"I'm waiting for someone."

"Oh, I'm sorry, Patrick."

"Don't be. She'll be here in a few minutes. Can I buy you a drink?"

" Will your date get mad at you for talking to me?"

Patrick ogled her in the black dress. "Maybe, but sitting here with you will make me seem more desirable."

"Silly games, Patrick. I don't know if I approve."

He gave her a big grin. "We're colleagues, Rosa. We need to help each other out."

They were laughing and having fun when a petite brunette took Patrick's arm and gave Rosa a wide-eyed look. Patrick introduced the girls and then led his date to the restaurant area. "Happy New Year, Rosa. I will see you at the ADA meeting in January."

She then noticed Dr. Ryan sitting at the end of the bar after Patrick left and picked up her drink to join him. "It was nice of you to invite us to dinner, Dr. Ryan. This is a lively place."

"Please call me Gerry."

"And call me Rosa." She smiled. "I thought you left for the evening."

"No, I just walked my staff to the parking lot to ensure they got home safely. I'm afraid they overindulged. Thank goodness they had the sense to have a friend pick them up."

He looked at Rosa and noticed she had another drink. "Are you sober enough to drive?"

"I'm fine. I just stepped in to see what the pub was like."

"Me too."

Rosa seized the moment. His hand was on the bar, and she put her hand over his. He didn't move but seemed surprised and needed a moment to collect his thoughts. After a pause, he gave her an apologetic look. "Rosa, I have something to tell you."

She could feel it coming, the dread, the embarrassment–she immediately sensed she had made a wrong move. She tried to make light of it. "Don't tell me, you have a wife, a girlfriend."

"No, Rosa."He hesitated. "I have a boyfriend." He was uncomfortable, but continued. "I would appreciate your discretion. My personal life could affect my professional status."

"Of course," she whispered. She felt sorry for him, knowing he didn't want to tell or hurt her feelings. The moment was awkward, but she appreciated his honesty.

He smiled. "You are a beautiful woman, Rosa, attractive in so many ways. If inclined to date women, you would be the one I would pick. I'm flattered."

Then Rosa remembered Chrissy's advice. Even an unavailable guy would appreciate the interest. Knowing the truth would save them from misunderstandings, and they could be friends. She withdrew her hand. "I'm sorry I had the wrong idea."

"Nothing to worry about; I admire you, Rosa, and I really like you. I look forward to next year and hope that together we can establish the dental clinic and make it a success."

Dr. Ryan finished his beer and seemed ready to go home. Rosa wanted to stay and insisted he leave her there. She told him she had friends at the pub and would like to visit. Rosa used this excuse to buy another drink; she wanted to numb the growing sense that the singles scene was not for her. The concept of going to bars to meet men was discouraging, and the reality of the holiday season was apparent; everyone had someone but her. The man she dreamt about turned out to be gay. Her newfound freedom was not so glamorous after all.

She sensed him before she saw him. He placed his hand on the back of her chair. When she turned, he smiled; he was so incredibly sexy.

"Did you enjoy the class?"

She gazed into his dreamy blue eyes. "I did. I am in much better shape since I returned to dance. Your teaching style was brilliant; you broke us down and then built us back up. It was like being in the Marines."

"Oh God, I'm sorry," he whispered. "That was not my intent. I was abrupt because I was nervous about teaching the class." He paused. "We haven't really met."

"I'm Rosa."

"Hi Rose. I never had a chance to talk to you in class. Can I buy you a drink?"

She knew she should not have another drink, but if she accepted, she could continue to talk to him.

"Ok."

Alex felt drawn to this woman. Her eyes were captivating, and a familiarity made him comfortable talking to her.

"So, Rose, what do you do?"

"I work at a dental office. But I would rather not talk about work."

"Okay, we won't talk about work. Let's talk about–us."

She couldn't help but notice he was looking at her legs and marveled at his interest. He had seen her in a leotard throughout the entire semester.

"That dress is incredible."

"I'm glad you like it because I like you."

He tried to stifle a smile. She realized the alcohol had made her a little too honest. The place was getting crowded and noisy. When he thought she could hear him, he finally answered. "I like you too, Rose. I'd like you even without the dress." He blushed; the comment came out wrong. "What I mean to say is, you don't need that dress to look your best." Another stupid comment.

Rosa just smiled. He was a notorious womanizer. Of course, he would be upfront about what he wanted from her.

"Listen, Rose, I'm sure you have the wrong impression of me."

She didn't correct him about her name. It didn't matter. She was sure that nothing would come of this flirtation. She decided to change the subject.

"I saw The Nutcracker and thought you were marvelous."

"Oh God, my most outrageous role. I hope it amused you."

"It did. I attended the performance with my mother, who let it slip she thought you were hot even with that mouse head on."

"She said that?"

"Not exactly. She commented, *"I can see why there are so many young ladies in his class."*

"That's funny. Does your mom have a sense of humor?"

"Not really. I think she was serious."

They couldn't stop smiling at each other, but the place was getting so loud it became difficult to talk. Rosa took his hand and pulled him toward her.

"I'd like to get to know you, Alex, but I can't hear."

He gave her a sexy smile. "Your place or mine?" he said jokingly.

"Which is closer?" she asked.

He was stunned by the ridiculous question. He had no idea where she lived; he had just learned her name a few minutes earlier. Alex answered honestly. "I imagine my place is since I walked."

She took his hand as they ventured into the chilly night air. He was astounded. She was luring him to his own house. He didn't believe she was serious, but wanted to see what would happen next. A full moon lit the way through the neighborhood. Alex was certain this was not a good idea, but he tended to follow through with bad ideas. He tried to rationalize. He couldn't allow her to drive, and he was in no condition to drive her home. Some random guy could pick her up if he left her at the bar, and she was safer with him than a stranger. They walked three blocks to his place; the night was clear, the sky romantic. He led her up the steps of his brick house. Soft lights were on in the living room so he wouldn't disturb Buster when he got home. Buster had his blanket on and was tucked in for the night. The luminescent glow of the fiber-optic Christmas tree gave the room a warm and romantic holiday feel. With Rosa in the room, the atmosphere was romantic. He took her coat and hung it in the hall closet. Once again, he admired her in the black dress and black sandals. He gazed at her back; so beautiful. He led her toward the living room couch.

"Can I get you something to drink? Coffee, ginger ale, water?"

"Ginger ale sounds nice."

But when he walked to the kitchen, she followed. She was nervous.

"You must be thirsty," he joked.

"I am." Then she looked at him with serious consideration. "Alex, you should not feel obligated to me; I mean, I don't expect anything to happen. I will hate it if you feel pressured; I know your reputation."

Her comments amused him. She was not serious about having an intimate rendezvous, but he couldn't resist the urge to tease her. "I assure you I can be discreet. It's up to you what happens next."

"You don't mind my being here?"

"No, Rose, I don't mind at all. You are welcome to stay. Since we have been drinking, it would be a good idea. No strings attached."

The concept of 'no strings attached' intrigued Rosa. He was so handsome and polite, and he was not asking anything of her. She was lonely and unsure of herself. She had an irrepressible desire to kiss him, so she asked, "Would you mind giving me a kiss, Alex?"

He smiled again and decided to challenge her. "Since you asked, I think you should kiss me."

She moved closer to him and gave him a sweet, gentle kiss. But it didn't end. It became deeper, less innocent, increasingly passionate, and they savored the interaction. As the kissing and touching continued, he pressed her against the kitchen counter and leaned into her. Realizing he wanted her empowered her to be bold.

"Would you like to sit on the couch?" he asked.

"No, I'd like to stay in the kitchen."

"Okay, but I must warn you, the kitchen is the most dangerous room in the house."

"And why is that?"

"Because it can get so incredibly hot in here."

Alex couldn't keep his hands off her and sensed this might not stop. And then, she gently moved away from him. She was having second thoughts, and though he felt frustrated, he was not sorry he had kissed her. It had been ages since he had experienced such an overwhelming attraction to a girl. He tried to cool off with a sip of ginger ale. She watched his movements. She hesitated. He gave her an apologetic smile even though she was the one to start the caress. When she slipped her dress off and laid it on the kitchen counter, her underthings were black and lacey, and he suddenly felt like he couldn't breathe. He knew she would be more attractive without the dress.

Rosa longed for him and evaluated her situation. He was the most amazing man; handsome and sexy, and there was a seductive gentleness about him that made him irresistible. She realized the intent was for one night, but she didn't care; she would always have the experience of being his lover, and she needed him desperately. Rosa misinterpreted his hesitation. She, already rejected by one man, didn't think her heart could take a rejection by Alex. He stammered a bit as he gazed at her. "Rose, I don't normally bring women to my place, and I don't have anything to protect you. And you should be afraid of me. I'm no gentleman."

"I'm covered, Alex. And right now, I'm not looking for a gentleman."

Despite his notorious reputation, he had never brought a woman home from a bar. But this time he couldn't help himself; he wanted her. She studied his demeanor and felt he needed more encouragement. She slipped off her panties and left them on the kitchen floor. The move hit him like a bolt of lightning; it knocked him off his feet, and as he knelt in front of her, he didn't know how it had happened. She was running her fingers through his hair. His lips searched her intimately, and he seduced her. She longed for his touch and begged him to take her. Alex had never been so overwhelmed with desire. She enticed all of his senses: her beauty, the rose scent in her hair, her quiet gasps of pleasure, and the way she felt when he was inside her. They moved onto the couch. Rosa wanted to please him more than anything. Their movements were a rewarding, intimate dance where every touch headed toward fulfillment and surrender. They danced at the edge of the stage for a long time, and he didn't know how long he could continue before he flung himself into the orchestra pit. Alex sensed she was a woman who could give herself completely. He felt her hunger, her need, and as he subtly shifted her to the top, he said exactly what she needed to hear.

"Rose, you're amazing; this is amazing. I want to give you everything, and I want you to give everything. Just let go."

And then it happened-the release of an underlying passion set free, a seismic revelation. Soft waves of unspeakable pleasure pulsed through her core, and then she felt so hot inside she thought she would explode. He felt her overwhelming physical response to him; she could not contain her soft cries even though she tried to. Her pleasure was inherent and involuntary, and his response to her, so powerful. After his release, he felt content, and captured by the beautiful woman in his arms. They were breathless. They remained in a comfortable embrace and did not want to move. The occasional aftershocks he felt from her led him to believe she was not done with him. Finally, he broke the silence.

"I don't intend to be forward, Rose, but would you like to move to the bedroom?"

She smiled. "I would like that, but does it seem too fast?"

"I promise you, Rose, it won't be fast."

The comment filled her with fire and anticipation. He picked her up and carried her to his room. Rosa looked longingly at his bed. A large double window was beside it, and moonlight was streaming onto the mattress. The sheets, pillow, and quilt were white, and when he placed her on the bed, it felt like being on a cloud. The bedding was seductively turned down. He unbuckled her sandals, then she slipped under the cool white sheets and waited for him. He wanted her with a fierce intensity and kissed her passionately. She ached for him and was more than ready. As he immersed himself in her warmth, they made love freely and fully, without thought, without hesitation. Rosa felt so alive. And once again they surrendered to each other in a finale that left them physically and emotionally spent. He stroked her hair and whispered,

"It's never been like this, Rose."

She wanted to believe him. They held onto each other as they fell into a deep and satisfied sleep.

Chapter 12

The early morning sunlight filtered through the double window, and Rosa opened her eyes. A strong male arm curled possessively around her waist. Alex. She couldn't believe she had spent a magnificent night with an extraordinary lover. Then she remembered bits of their conversation, and one comment stood out: *'No strings attached.'* She had to leave; following a memorable night with an awkward morning would be anticlimactic. He slept soundly as she slipped out of his warm, cozy embrace. Rosa was cold and naked. It was drafty in the house, and there was nothing in the bedroom to use as a cover. Alex was wrapped up in the comforter, and there were no clothes in the bedroom. She remembered her coat hung in the hall closet. She tiptoed into the hallway and slipped on her warm coat.

Rosa noticed an intricate sampler on the wall; a scene from the Garden of Eden. Rosa felt a pang of guilt and imagined it was there for a reason. It was a surprise that Alex would be religious, but there were religious references everywhere, and she was concerned that she led him astray. She invited herself over, then threw herself at him in a way that would be difficult for any healthy young male to resist. She lured him, tempted him, and threw her clothes off in front of him. Only then did he take action. He did not seem to be the smooth operator she had heard rumors about. Then again, it could be part of the seduction. She found her dress on the kitchen counter and panties on the kitchen floor. '*Oh God'*, she thought, *'I was the temptress and the apple.'* She was distraught when she couldn't find her bra, but it was hidden in the couch cushions. She straightened the couch and stuffed the bra in her purse. As she searched for her sandals, she remembered how he had carefully removed them before he made love to her a second time. She slipped into his room and found them placed neatly at the foot of the bed.

Rosa spent a moment admiring her new lover. Alex seemed comfortable and content, and she lingered as she savored the vision of him sleeping. He had a square jawline, was unshaven, and looked very masculine, but beautiful too because of his thick blond curls and long lashes. He was God's gift to women; the world's greatest lover. Rosa had to protect her heart; he was not the type to become a serious boyfriend, and she should not get attached. But it was too late. She was attached. She grabbed her shoes and headed for the door. It didn't seem right to vanish without a word, but she didn't want him to feel obligated to call her. She left a note on the kitchen table but did not leave her phone number. She silently slipped past his bedroom, walked into the common hallway shared with the upstairs tenants, and cautiously studied the lock leading to the outside. There was a deadbolt and a key, and there appeared to be an alarm system. The last thing she wanted was to trigger an alarm and wake everyone up. She turned the key and was relieved it opened without incident. She ventured into the frosty morning air.

It was Christmas Eve, but so early in the morning that all seemed quiet. She wore her skimpy dress with sandals and no stockings, and her overcoat barely kept her warm enough for the brisk walk to her car. She could hear traffic on the main street and knew she could find Mother's Pub even though she was unaware of her surroundings the night before. A brisk wind and temperatures below freezing assaulted her bare legs. As she located her car in the restaurant parking lot, she breathed a sigh of relief; the car started immediately. She wondered if her roommates realized she was out all night.

When she got home, Rosa snuck in the back door and startled Connie in the kitchen. " I didn't expect you up this early," Rosa whispered. "It's Christmas Eve; aren't you off from work?"

"Believe it or not, they need me this morning. Would you like scrambled eggs and cheese?"

"Sure." Rosa was confused. "I thought you were out late with Charlie last night."

"He is upstairs sleeping. He's hungover after the bowling league's Christmas party and probably won't be up before noon. What about you, Rosa? How did it go with Dr. Ryan?"

"We are on a first-name basis now; I can call him Gerry. But it didn't work out with him."

"Where were you last night?"

"I spent the night with someone else."

"Oh, this is worth being late for work." Connie sat down and gave Rosa her full attention. "What happened?"

"Dr. Ryan had a nice dinner planned, but the women on his office staff were annoying. I was uncomfortable watching the office girls compete for his attention, and they were drinking too much. I barely had the chance to talk to him at dinner and decided to leave after a visit to the pub. That's when I spotted Patrick at the bar."

Connie cut in. "I thought you weren't interested in dating Patrick."

"I'm not. He was waiting for a date, but I sat down, and Patrick bought me a drink. When his dinner date arrived, she was not pleased to see him with me, and they immediately left for the restaurant. I suddenly realized Gerry was sitting at the other end of the bar. I made my move; it wasn't much of a move since I sat next to him and put my hand over his. He looked embarrassed and apologized if he had given me the wrong impression. Turns out he's gay."

"No ... you didn't have any idea?"

"None. All the single nurses at the hospital are wasting their time fantasizing about him. Just my luck, the man I picked out for myself is unavailable. I needed to drink after that."

"So where did you go last night?"

"Connie, I slept with my dance teacher."

She gasped. "Don't you like him?"

"I do, even more so after I slept with him. The story is very complex, since I had a crush on him in high school."

"Wait, you knew him from before?"

"We knew each other for less than a week. He doesn't remember me."

"Does he know now?"

"He will after reading my note."

Connie seemed confused. "You slept with him and spent the night, and still he didn't realize who you are?"

Rosa tried to explain. "My appearance changed drastically during my last two years of high school. Back then I was a young girl with limp brown hair and braces. Deep down I think he sensed a connection; we were so comfortable with intimacy. When we touched, it was clear we were not strangers. We danced together while I vacationed at a ranch in upper New York State, but he didn't remember that. I'm sure he assumed I was familiar because I spent the semester in his jazz class."

"Are you going to see him again?"

"Probably not. I left while he was sleeping, and I didn't leave my number. He doesn't know my last name."

"Are you disappointed?"

"That's the problem, Connie; I'm overwhelmed with the elation I felt after spending the night. It's like the fantasy I never knew I had. He was amazing."

"I hope you know what you're doing, Rosa. If it was that memorable for you, it was good for him as well, and I bet he wants to see you again. Why did you leave?"

"Last night he said, '*No strings attached,*' and I have to assume he meant it. Doesn't that sound like a one-night proposition?"

Connie shrugged her shoulders. "I guess, but you may have misunderstood."

***

Alex awakened from a deep sleep with a knock at his front door. He could have sworn he fell asleep with his arms around a tall blond. He detected a faint rose scent as he grasped her pillow. She was real. He slipped on his sweatpants and stumbled to the front door.

"Russ?"

"Al, don't look so surprised. You're the one who wanted me over early. What's the matter? You never sleep in."

"I'm sorry, Russ. I forgot all about the plumbing appointment."

"Rough night? You look hungover."

"Maybe a little."

"Sit. I didn't have coffee this morning; I'll make a pot." Nana's house was like a second home to Russ. He started the coffee, then noticed a shiny object on the floor. "Does this belong to you, Al?" It was an earring shaped like a Christmas present. He gave his cousin a suspicious look. "I thought you never brought girls over here."

"I never did. Last night was a first."

" Who is she?"

"The tall blond I admired in jazz class."

"What happened?"

"I don't know. She left."

"Oh, that's not good, Al."

Alex gave him a weary glance. "I can't understand it; we had an amazing night together. I fell asleep dreaming about what I would make her for breakfast."

"Just call her up."

"I don't have her number, and I didn't ask for her last name."

"Think about it, Alex. She was in your jazz class, and Jackie has her information. It shouldn't be difficult to contact her." Russ handed the coffee to Alex and felt sorry for him. He knew what it was like to be dismissed by a woman.

"It would be awkward to ask Jackie, but I could find out. Still, I don't understand what happened."

"Take a look around, Al. We don't notice it, but the place looks like the church rectory. She might have felt guilty about last night. What did you do?"

Alex sighed. "Everything ... we did everything and more than once."

Russ felt uncomfortably flushed by the comment. "I think we should look at that leaky pipe."

"Right. It's next to the washing machine."

They brought the coffee downstairs and headed for the washer. The laundry had piled up. As Russ diagnosed the problem, they heard shuffling at the top of the stairs. "Lawrence, be careful of the steps."

The little boy navigated the steep stairs and approached Alex. "You forgot to uncover Buster this morning. I heard him chirping and removed his blanket, then gave him fresh water."

"Thanks, Lawrence."

Russ continued to work on the plumbing. He tried to explain the oversight. "Alex doesn't feel good this morning."

The boy gave him a thoughtful look. "Was that lady a nurse?"

"What lady?" asked Russ.

"The lady who was in the hall this morning. I think she didn't know how to work the lock."

Alex became more alert. "Did you talk to her, Lawrence?"

"No, she didn't see me. Was she a nurse?"

"Just a friend." Alex shot Russ a dirty look. Russ could barely compose himself.

"Like a sleepover?" asked Lawrence.

Russ broke out in a hearty laugh, which he quickly controlled. "Sorry, Lawrence, I just thought of a funny joke."

Alex made a weak attempt at damage control. "Listen, buddy, this is guy talk; we don't have to discuss it with Nana or your mom."

"Why not, Alex?"

"Well, it's embarrassing." He noticed the boy's questioning look and tried to explain. "I like that lady but don't know if she wants to be my girlfriend. I feel bad about it, and would like it to be a secret."

" I won't tell Mom. I know how to keep secrets from her."

"No, Lawrence, it's not right to keep secrets from your mother. But if a friend tells you something personal, you can keep it to yourself, as long as it's not wrong or dangerous. That's what buddies do."

"I understand Alex. I won't say anything." Suddenly he looked antsy. "What time is it?"

"Almost nine o'clock."

"At nine, I'm allowed to turn on the TV." The little guy started running up the steps.

"Be careful, Lawrence."

Russ finished the repair and followed Alex up the stairs. He sat on the couch in the living room. "Al, are you going to be alright?"

"No; I can't believe she just left."

Russ noticed a paper on the coffee table and gave it to Alex. "What is it?"

"A note."

"With her number?"

"No, it's a kind of thank-you note."

Russ once again couldn't contain his laughter. "Alex, only you could get a thank-you note for sex. Wait until I tell my bowling buddies."

"You wouldn't."

Russ shrugged. "What does it say?"

"Dear Curly," read Alex, "I know there was a reason I went to that bar. You were wonderful; I won't forget last night. Thank you. Rosie."

Russ was astonished; he had known Rosie from the ranch in the summer of 1972. "You slept with Rosie? Didn't you know?"

"I should have, since she seemed so familiar; she even felt familiar. Her appearance has changed since she's a grown woman now. No wonder she left."

"You had eyes for each other ten years ago. I guess she needed to finish what you started."

Alex gave Russ a desperate look. "I don't know if I'll ever be finished."

Russ stopped laughing and sympathized with Alex. His cousin had it bad.

Chapter 13

Alex spent Christmas Day with Nana at the rehab facility and brought holiday cheer to the residents. Nana recovered from her broken hip and expected to remain at the facility for the full stay allowed by Medicare. She was determined to walk independently and exerted herself during physical therapy. Decisions about her care had to be made, and Alex wondered if he would hire a caregiver for her after she finished. He worried that he couldn't afford the expense and would have to take a second mortgage on the house. He did not want to think about finances on Christmas Day. Alex brought his boombox with holiday tunes and became the impromptu coordinator of activities. He wore a Santa hat and distributed gifts to the residents; he initiated games and dancing, and even the elderly men in the facility had to smile. They remembered what it was like to be twenty-eight years old, healthy, and full of enthusiasm. The women, of course, adored him.

He continued to look for Rosa whenever he was out with Russ or in a public place. He believed in fate and knew the night they spent together couldn't be the end. New Year's Eve was a bust. Alex and Russ returned home from Mother's Pub, drunk and sad. January and February would be bleak, like the cold, harsh winter weather.

Rosa, Patrick, and Rebecca met for the ADA meeting every month. A blizzard hit the tri-state area in February, and the Dental Association canceled the meeting. Rosa missed the opportunity to see Rebecca, so she asked her out to brunch. They met at the 'Tic Tock Diner.' After a perfect cup of coffee, they relaxed and enjoyed a rare encounter without Patrick or the other ADA members. Eating at a New Jersey diner was a unique experience, and Rosa had spent years in the Midwest yearning for a diner breakfast. Rosa was interested in Rebecca's work environment.

"How is the job with Dr. Sabarini?"

"We're busy, and I enjoy working with him. Sometimes I feel like the granddaughter he never had."

"I'm surprised he is not in the ADA. I bet he knows most of the members."

"Dr. Sabarini is a bit of a rebel," noted Rebecca. "He challenged the ADA and left years ago, something about dental insurance."

"Why would he have reservations about dental insurance?"

"He thinks of it as third-party interference between the doctor and the patient. Dr. Sabarini predicts that insurance companies will start offering generous terms, but as time goes on and patients depend on insurance, they will decrease benefits and raise premiums. He sees insurance as callous and profit-driven, with little or no regard for the patient's health."

"I work in an insurance office every day," replied Rosa. "Most of the patients don't know what they have, and the expectations of coverage and the reality of what is covered are different. Very deceptive."

Both women were concerned about their careers. "Have you heard about the virus?" asked Rosa.

"Yes, and it's scary. At first, it was only gay men, but they recently found cases transmitted through blood transfusions and infected needles."

"It makes one more cautious about dating in this environment."

"Never mind dating, what about work? It's transmitted through blood, so what about saliva? Is it present in aerosols produced by the dental handpiece? We could be risking our lives just by doing our jobs. I told Dr. Sabarini I intend to wear gloves, a mask, and protective eyewear. He agreed, though he doesn't intend to change."

"I didn't sign up for this."

"Neither did I. The dating issue is not a concern for me, as I have been celibate for years."

Rosa waited for an explanation.

"I fell in love senior year, and I haven't been able to get past it."

"What happened?"

"I graduated, but he is still in school. His name is Anthony. I still write to him sometimes."

"Is it Anthony Roselli?"

"Yes, do you know him?"

"I only met him once; he was bartending at a jazz club. I can understand why he's hard to forget."

"How did he look?"

"He was busy at the bar, but funny when I spoke to him. He joked in a self-deprecating way."

"That sounds like Anthony. I still miss him."

Rosa admitted she was lonely too. "I dated a medical student for years, but he did not want to commit. After graduation, we went our separate ways. Perhaps breaking up with him was a mistake."

"So you have been celibate too?"

"Not exactly. I slept with my dance teacher once."

"What happened with that?"

"Nothing. I left after spending the night with him. Unfortunately, he's the one I can't seem to forget."

***

Alex finally took Russ's advice and visited the studio. Fred Donovan was in the business office, and after saying hello, Alex asked for the list of students from last semester's jazz class. Fred eyed him suspiciously, but brought out the list.

" When you took the semester off, the students were disappointed. I understand that Nana has to get settled before you commit to any more classes, but Jackie and I hope you will teach in the future. We see real value in adding adult classes to the schedule. These clients could take lessons for years; they will not leave like the young dancers who either lose interest in high school or leave when they go to college."

"I realize it is a business, Fred. If you're worried about the list, I promise it won't be used to promote anything outside of Donovan Studio. If anything, I will contact students to see if there is interest in summer classes here."

"Here you go, Alex; the list. I have names and phone numbers, and if they paid by check, I have an address too. Let me know if you want to start a class. As you know, the studio is usually empty in the summer."

Alex reviewed the names, which seemed to be God's cruel joke. Rosemary, Roseann, Rosalinda, Rosette, and Rose were names on the roster. He regretted his failure to befriend the students in his jazz class. He could not think of an excuse to call them. Jackie waved to Alex before he left the studio. She met Fred at the business office. "Did Alex talk to you about coming back?" she asked.

"Unfortunately, no. He wanted the jazz class list, and I suspect he was not being candid about his motive."

Jackie couldn't hide her smile. "If I know our Alex, he was looking for information about Rosalinda. He had his eye on her all semester."

"The tall blond?"

"Yes, and he may return asking more questions. That class roster is not helpful. There are too many women named Rose."

"I see his dilemma." sighed Fred. "We owe Alex a favor after spreading those salacious rumors, which, by the way, have backfired. It promoted our business, since Alex's mystery and intrigue brought many curious women to the jazz class. But for Alex, it has been a curse. Some women dismiss him as a dating prospect because of his reputation."

"That was an unintended consequence of our actions. At least they know he's not gay."

Fred was concerned. "Jackie, was unethical to give him the list?"

"Maybe, but who's to know? Alex would never force the issue. He's not the type to impose his affections on someone who is not interested. By the way, did you ask about the showcase?"

"No, I have to call him. I forgot."

Alex looked at the list, discouraged but not defeated. He had a feeling he would run into her. If all else failed, offering a summer master class could reveal her identity. He might figure out who she was even if she chose not to enroll. He was certain he would recognize her voice. That night was forever seared into his memory.

Chapter 14

The patients at Rosa's nursing home job enjoyed their hygiene visits, kept their appointments, and were appreciative. Dottie was busy with patient scheduling and Medicaid claims. She was doing a wonderful job. Rosa loved the position, the patients, and working with Dottie, but the compensation was meager and slow to come in. Medicaid regularly denied payments because of ridiculous requests for documentation. Rosa performed only basic dentistry on these patients and could not understand why any claim needed a follow-up explanation. Rosa's purpose was to help patients, and she resigned herself to the slow and complicated process of getting paid by Medicaid. Working with Dottie and meeting with Dr. Ryan was a pleasant change from her hectic schedule at Dental Connections, so she valued the experience and overlooked the problems with monetary compensation. Her professional relationship with Dr.Ryan was becoming a friendship. He arrived one evening after hours, when she was evaluating claims. He seemed hesitant to approach her.

"Hi Rosa, you're here late this evening."

"I stayed to resubmit these insurance denials. There are certain codes they question, and we have to avoid using them."

"I hate playing insurance games. The problem is that the people processing the claims are not doctors." Dr. Ryan stood there for a moment and seemed to collect his thoughts. Finally, he revealed his reason for stopping in.

"My friend in New York is having a gala to raise money for the new cardiology wing at his hospital. He was instrumental in completing the project, and invited me to attend. I would love to see him and contribute to this fundraiser. Would you like to go with me?"

She hesitated. "Gerry, are you sure your partner won't mind?"

"He is a homebody, rarely seen in a dress shirt, and this is a fancy black-tie event. He doesn't want to go. There will be dinner and dancing, and I'm sure Art would be happy that I have someone to go with."

"Sounds like fun, Gerry. What should I wear?"

"That black dress was intriguing."

He noticed my dress; she thought. That surprised her.

"Don't you think I should be more conservative?"

"I appreciate having an attractive woman on my arm, and I don't see any point in concealing your beauty. You should wear an outfit that makes you feel like the alluring woman you are. I hope you like to dance, as they have hired an orchestra."

Rosa understood his motives; he wanted to have a fun date, and since she knew his preferences, he would not have to worry about a misunderstanding. It was unfortunate that he felt the need to hide his partner. She looked forward to the event. He would be even more handsome in formal attire, and they would make a stunning couple. She shopped and found a midnight blue silk dress that was flattering. It fell below the knee but had a slit on the side; low in the back, much like her black dress. She had a fleeting recollection of Alex admiring her back. Most men would concentrate their attention elsewhere.

***

The night air was bitterly cold when Gerry picked her up for the gala, but this time Rosa wore stockings. Her elegant pumps matched the dress; they made her appear taller than her date, but she suspected he would like that. It was refreshing how relaxed they were since there were no expectations. Gerry loved to dance. They were the first couple on the dance floor, and other couples soon joined them because of their enthusiasm. After a few quick speeches and a toast, the salad was served, and Rosa felt tipsy from the champagne. She swore she had heard a familiar voice but dismissed the notion since she did not know anyone from the hospital or who lived in New York. She could not hide her surprise when she looked up. Yale was standing before her.

"Hello, Rosa. You look beautiful as ever."

She tried to compose herself. He had seen her on the dance floor with Gerry. Although blindsided, her professional poise handled the surprise. "Hello Yale, this is my date, Gerry Ryan." She touched Gerry's arm and looked toward Yale. "My friend from college, Yale Dixon."

The men shook hands, but it was not friendly. Yale looked possessive, and Gerry was calm but cautious. Yale continued. "I didn't expect to see you at a hospital event in New York City. I am a resident here."

Gerry intervened. "Dr. Patel is a friend from medical school. We are here at his invitation."

Yale looked uncomfortable, since Rosa's date was a friend of his boss. "Gerry, I hope you don't mind if I dance with Rosa after dinner."

Gerry wavered. "That's totally up to her."

Rosa smiled. "I'll dance with you later, Yale."

When Yale left, she gave Gerry a brief explanation. "I dated Yale for six years. He did not include me in his plans following graduation, so I broke up with him last spring. That was less than a year ago, so the feelings are still raw."

Gerry frowned. "I don't want to interfere in any way. What do you want me to do?"

Rosa gazed at her handsome date. Though embarrassed, she was brutally honest about what she wanted from him. "I want to get over Yale, and I don't want to reconcile. I think you should act like you like me."

"But I do like you."

"You know what I mean."

"So shall I act like I hope to see you without the dress?"

"Exactly."

"Well, I don't have to pretend. I know the genuine beauty lies within the dress."

After dinner, his dancing became more intimate and seductive. Gerry knew how to showcase a partner, and his steamy moves gave the impression that they were involved. Rosa tried to dampen the attraction she felt when in his arms. He was perfect for her in every way except one, and she found it difficult to accept that he was unavailable. Because he was drinking, she stopped; she assumed she would have to drive, and she had to keep her wits about her when she danced with Yale, who finally asked late in the evening. Yale was uncomfortable dancing, and Rosa was certain he forced himself onto the dance floor so he could talk to her. Annoyed at her partnership with Gerry, Yale held her a little closer than he should have.

"So, Rosa, do you have any regrets?"

Rosa did not want to answer. Seeing him again was heartbreaking. Finally, she answered. "You wouldn't commit, Yale."

"You didn't give me a chance." He looked over at Gerry. "What is going on with that guy?"

"He is the attending physician where I work. He started the dental clinic, and we are friends."

"Are you sleeping with him?"

"That's none of your business, Yale."

The dance and the conversation were over. She looked shaken as she walked back to Gerry.

"Are you upset, Rosa?"

"I'm fine, but ready to go."

"I'm ready too, but I don't think I should drive."

"I'll take over, Gerry. I'm sorry that I drove you to drink."

"No need to apologize. I enjoyed myself. It has been a long time since I danced with a woman. It was exciting."

Rosa worried about how she would handle the rest of the evening. She was emotional. When she drove Gerry to her house, she intended to keep him there until morning. She could not allow him to take a chance on the road. It was past midnight, and the house was quiet. Rosa brought him into the kitchen and made coffee, in case he insisted on leaving. Gerry was tired and upset.

"What's wrong?" she asked.

"I'm a lousy drunk, Rosa. I have a high for a few hours, then I always sink into a deep depression. I can't escape the despair. My friends are getting sick. Healthy, vibrant men suddenly sick from this damned virus. It is so unfair, and there is no cure."

"Are you worried about yourself and Art?"

"We have been in an exclusive relationship for a couple of years, and doubt we are at risk. But a friend from college presented with Kaposi's sarcoma, then AIDS. He is wasting away."

Gerry started crying. Rosa put her arms around him. "Please keep safe, Gerry. You are a wonderful doctor, and you can help these patients. The residents of the nursing home need you. I need you." The alcohol had fueled his emotional outburst. He was in no shape to drive.

"You can stay in my room tonight, and I'll take the couch. Please don't worry about my roommates; they know our situation." She brought him to her room and hung up his suit jacket. He slipped off his trousers and collapsed onto her bed. She brushed his hair with her warm touch. Rosa wondered why life had to be so complicated. She felt compassion for Gerry and his friends and prayed they would be safe, and that a cure would soon be available.

In the morning, Rosa heard Connie tiptoe past the couch. When Rosa went upstairs, Gerry was ready to leave. His behavior after the gala embarrassed him. Rosa insisted he join her for coffee and breakfast, and they met Connie in the kitchen. Rosa described the fun they had dancing at the gala. Gerry seemed comfortable conversing with Connie, who had a way of making guests feel welcome. Rosa almost forgot he was a doctor and her administrator at work. She was used to the calm and confident Dr. Ryan at the hospital, but he was as insecure as everyone else and felt helpless when confronted with this disease that had no cure. He was a wonderful man; sensitive and easy to get along with. She valued his friendship and was sorry she would not have a romantic relationship with him. It would be easy to fall in love with him.

Chapter 15

Yale could not erase the image of Rosa and Gerry Ryan on the dance floor, and wondered if they were seriously involved. Rosa liked tall men, but Gerry was shorter than her. He was the polar opposite of Yale; calm, accommodating, and soft-spoken. Rosa and Gerry seemed comfortable holding each other, like lovers. The intimacy was obvious when they danced, and Yale felt sick when he thought about it. Dr. Ryan was well-established, wealthy, and smart enough to hold on to Rosa, who was so desirable. She was an unspoiled beauty; smart, hard-working, and reliable. He recognized these qualities when he first asked her out. She had given him her virginity and her devotion, and he assumed she would follow him everywhere. But he took her for granted, and his family's opinion clouded his judgment. Her dedication to dentistry surprised him. He did not think she would follow through with her career.

It didn't take her long to find someone else. Ryan was a lucky bastard when the most perfect woman appeared at his hospital. Yale knew it would be difficult to compete, but she did not have a ring on her finger and she did not introduce Gerry as her boyfriend. The following day, Yale called her and left a message on her answering machine. *"Hi Rosa, this is Yale. I'm sorry about the way I acted last night; I guess I was jealous seeing you with the other doctor. I am working in New York and would love to take you out. Give me a call, please. By the way, I miss you."*

Rosa did not call back and wondered how he had obtained her phone number. It hurt to hear his voice on the answering machine. She missed having a boyfriend, but memories from last year strengthened her resolve to avoid him. His family had given her a cool reception, and she was deeply troubled by his behavior on Valentine's Day. She wondered where he was the day they broke up, who he was with, and why he didn't call. The truth is, she stopped trusting him, and she did not think she could ever trust him again.

***

Rosa and Dottie were busy at the nursing home. Freezing rainstorms ruined dental office schedules, but the patients at the nursing home were already in-house and did not have to worry about driving to their appointments. There were few surprises in the schedule, so when Rosa finished her day early in the afternoon, Gerry was often there to ask her out for a late lunch. It seemed their friendship was stronger after the night at the gala. She felt free to talk about her loneliness and about Yale. Gerry did not like the guy, but kept his feelings to himself. His attraction to Rosa confused him, and he wondered if it affected his perspective. Rosa would have to make the right choices on her own.

By midweek, the hygienist at Dental Connections had called in sick, so Rosa had to take some of the hygiene appointments. Dawn was certified to take X-rays, polish, and administer fluoride treatments, and they worked as a team to accommodate all the patients. One little guy made an impression; his upper central incisors were missing, and Rosa thought this mixed dentition stage was adorable. When she introduced herself, he had a big smile on his face.

"Hello Lawrence; I'm Dr. Fletcher. How are your teeth?" Lawrence didn't answer but gave her a bigger smile. "I can see you are a good patient. I will sit you back so I can count your teeth."

Finally, he spoke up. "Mommy, I'm old enough to visit the dentist by myself. You can get me later."

Rosa, Dawn, and Tammy smiled at the odd request. Dawn spoke up to reassure his mom. "I will bring Lawrence to the reception area when we are done. If you have questions, Dr. Fletcher will meet you at the front desk."

Rosa cleaned his teeth and taught him proper brushing and flossing. He looked at Dawn while she was in the back preparing his fluoride treatment. She wasn't paying attention. He whispered to Rosa, "Don't worry, I didn't say anything."

Rosa had no idea what he was talking about, so she waited for his next comment. He continued. "About the sleepover, I know it's a secret, so I didn't tell Mom."

Dawn had her back to them but was concerned, and so was Rosa. His next comment nearly knocked Rosa off her chair. "I think you should be Alex's girlfriend."

Rosa turned several shades of red as Dawn stared at her. Rosa looked at his chart and realized he had the same address as Alex and must be the upstairs tenant. She was honest with her little patient.

"Lawrence, I do like Alex, but I'm not his girlfriend."

"That's too bad," he sighed."He told me he likes you."

Dawn rescued Dr. Fletcher from further inquiry. "Come with me, Lawrence. I'll give you a toothbrush, and you can choose a prize."

He followed Dawn, but not before giving Dr. Fletcher a thumbs up. Tammy was waiting at the front, relieved to hear Lawrence didn't have cavities. Rosa went to the consultation room to compose herself. When she returned to the treatment room, Dawn was disinfecting the dental chair and was not about to ignore what she had heard. Dawn folded her arms over her chest and demanded an explanation. "I heard everything, Dr. Fletcher. Give it up."

"Alex is my dance teacher, and I slept with him once." She wondered how many times she would have to confess.

"So how was it, and how does Lawrence know?"

"It was great, and I can only assume that Lawrence saw me leaving in the morning. He has the same address and must live upstairs."

"So what happened with Alex?"

"Nothing. I left."

"What? Did he call you afterward?"

"No, I didn't leave my number." Dawn looked at Rosa in disbelief. Then Rosa added, "But I did leave a thankyou note."

Dawn couldn't hide her laughter; the remark was funny, but sad. "Dr. Fletcher you're supposed to talk to the guy in the morning to figure out if he wants to see you again."

Rosa didn't have time to further her explanation. Everything seemed simple to Dawn, who was so confident. She was a few years older than Rosa, married and uninhibited. When she told Rosa she had a tattoo, Rosa asked where. Dawn pulled down her scrubs to expose the upper part of her buttocks. Tattooed on was a sunrise. "Do you get it?" she asked. "The crack of dawn." After that, Rosa saved all personal questions until after the patients had left for the day. They had a crazy working relationship, and since Dawn always provided the entertainment, Rosa could remain reserved in front of her patients.

Her assistant taught her to lighten up and make the patients feel less stressed.

At 5 o'clock, Rosa was happy to end her hectic day. She needed time to think. She felt a powerful longing and a heartache that surprised her when she thought about Alex. First, memories of Alex when he was eighteen years old, so kind and thoughtful. Then she experienced Alex at twenty-eight, so gentle and intense, and sure of the pleasure he could give to her. In both instances, he was there for her. She couldn't forget him.

Chapter 16

The floor plan and the clutter in the house would not accommodate a person with a walker, so Alex tried to remove hazards and make the residence safe for Nana. He did the best he could while she was at the rehabilitation facility. He discarded the old area rugs and left the hardwood floors bare, giving the space a simple appearance. Russ installed a bar for the handicapped in the bathroom. Alex spoke to Russ about installing a walk-in tub and shower. Then Nana shocked him with a change of plans.

"Alex, I'm sorry I didn't say something sooner, but your Aunt Mary has asked me to move in with her. She has a ranch and plenty of room; there are no steps inside, and she even has a handicap ramp outside. She has been lonely since Uncle Max passed away, and we can both live without financial worry if we combine our Social Security checks. If I move back in with you, my life will be restricted to a few rooms because of the stairs."

"Are you sure, Nana? What are you going to do with the house?"

"Alex, don't you understand that visit to the lawyer when you were eighteen? The house belongs to you."

"I thought that was a will."

"No, the house was a gift. I have tried to continue paying the mortgage to make life easy for you, but I can't afford it anymore. The upkeep and taxes have become too costly. But you are young and ambitious, and I'm sure you can own that house mortgage-free in a few years. I ask that you maintain the same rental rate for Tammy, since she is struggling to make ends meet."

Nana's generosity astounded Alex, but he was concerned about the rest of the family. "What do Russ and Megan think about this? You have two other grandchildren."

"Your cousins know. Russ and his sister have two parents and have had a stable upbringing. You have struggled to do without your whole life. They are happy that you have the house, and since your grandfather and I were your adopted parents, I feel obligated to you. I have left my retirement accounts to Russ and Megan so they will have something from me."

Alex felt guilty about owning the house, but knew it might be for the best. The place was close enough to Nana and Aunt Mary that he could help them out.

"There's only one problem," added Nana. "Mary doesn't want the bird in her house. She has allergies and thinks living with Buster could make her sick."

"No problem, Nana. Buster and I have become best buds."

"I noticed."

"His change in behavior concerns me. He misses you, and I am gone most of the day; he must be lonely. I may go to a pet store and get him a companion."

"To be honest, Alex, I have thought about that too. He sometimes gets so angry at that mirror. Even when his cage is clean and he has plenty of food and water, he seems frustrated."

"Do you think he would be happy with another bird?"

"I don't know, but he is friendly and enjoys company. He doesn't bite, and he might enjoy a companion as long as the other bird is not noisy or aggressive."

Alex did not want to discuss this with his grandmother, but he thought Buster needed a girlfriend. He would think about it later. His priority was Nana. She asked Alex if he wanted to keep the kitchen table and the living room couch. She planned to give away or donate everything else. Aunt Mary had plenty of room, but Nana did not want to clutter Mary's house with her belongings. Uncle Max had been a hoarder, and Mary had worked to clean the place after he died. They both needed it simple and easy to maintain, without hazards that could lead to another fall. Alex asked for a few wall hangings and the fiber optic Christmas tree. They held sentimental value for Alex, and he wanted to keep them for his family if he was fortunate enough to have one in the future. They used Russ's van and moved furniture right away. Nana's bedroom set, her clothes, and her most treasured knick-knacks were there for her at Aunt Mary's house when she left rehab. Alex was proud of Nana for accepting the transition; it was difficult for children of the Great Depression to part with their belongings.

***

Alex was so preoccupied with the move, he almost forgot about his appointment. He rushed over and arrived on time. He was a quick hygiene appointment, and Lynn, his hygienist, was happy to see him, an easy patient for the end of the day. She greeted him and explained that the office was short-staffed. "I hope you don't mind, but Dr.

Schwartz is sick this week. One of the other doctors will do your exam today."

"That's fine, but I will miss seeing the Doc. He always has jokes to tell."

After his X-rays and cleaning, Lynn checked to see which doctor was available for a quick exam. Dr. Fletcher had just finished her last patient of the day. As Rosa walked into the operatory, she stopped short, and her heart did a little flip when she saw the curly blond hair. She tried to compose herself and was grateful to have on her surgical mask. Alex recognized those beautiful, exotic eyes. He was flustered.

Rosa looked at Lynn. "You can do instruments while I take care of this exam. I will talk to the patient about his treatment plan."

Lynn gave Dr. Fletcher an odd look. There was no treatment plan since Alex needed no work. She hoped Dr. Fletcher would not suggest correcting the slight overlap of his right lateral incisor over his central incisor. She thought the imperfection gave his smile a sexy look. Without a word, Rosa completed the examination. When she moved the chair upright, he took her latex-gloved hand.

"Rose, we shouldn't be meeting like this. We have to talk."

"Not here," she whispered. Just then, Dawn peeked in the room, and a tall blond patient was holding Dr. Fletcher's hand. She pretended she didn't see it, but would, of course, ask about it later.

"I'm finished for the day, Alex. I can meet you at the pizzeria next door."

"I'll be counting the minutes," he replied.

Rosa hurried to the employee lounge, brushed her hair, and applied lip gloss. She wondered what she was doing. Gerry and Yale were vying for attention; she didn't need to add another complication. She owed Alex an explanation for her abrupt departure after their erotic night together. Even so, his timing was awful.

He ordered a pizza and two ginger ales. He remembered her name from the list, Rosalinda Fletcher. She was a doctor. No wonder she didn't take him seriously; she was probably looking for a professional man. There was no denying her strong physical attraction to him, and he wondered if she thought about their night together as he did. He doubted he could have the prestige of a doctor or dentist, but at least he owned a house. Of course, she didn't know that. He tried to formulate an alternate strategy if she hesitated to go out with him. As she joined him in the booth, they both appeared nervous. She sipped her ginger ale and smiled.

"I never did get the ginger ale you promised me."

The thought of that moment made him hot. He took her hand, and it felt so much better without the latex glove. "I always keep my promises. By the way, I thought you said your name was Rose. Is it Rosa or Rosie?"

"It's Rosa. It was so loud at Mother's that night you didn't hear me."

"Oh God. How could you stand me calling you the wrong name when so much was happening?"

Rosa felt flushed. "I didn't care what you called me, Alex. I needed that night with you."

He gazed into her eyes, trying to understand. They shared a moment of intimacy, but then she looked away.

"Why did you leave?" he whispered.

"Listen. Alex, my life is complicated, and I should be upfront with you."

He interrupted since he could not face rejection. "Wait, I know what you are going to say. Although I would love a repeat performance of our last encounter, that is not why I wanted to talk to you."

"It's not?"

"No, I want to discuss dancing."

Rosa waited. She couldn't imagine what she could do for him. He continued. "In May, there is a ballroom showcase I promised to do for the Donovans. It is at the Madison Hotel, and several studios will participate. The purpose is to recruit new students, so the timing is perfect for them since they are starting a ballroom program in the fall. They asked me to choreograph and perform three numbers, and I need a partner."

"But I am not a professional dancer. Surely you can find someone more qualified than me."

"I am not a professional ballroom dancer either, but I taught classes while in college. I could ask a woman in the company, but Ballroom looks best with the right size partner, and I'm too tall for them. We danced so well together years ago at the ranch."

Rosa was stunned by the offer to partner with Alex. Then the pizza arrived.

"Think it over, Rosa. It's only dancing. Of course, you're always welcome to come to my place; I'm redecorating and remember how anxious you were to see it last time."

Rosa turned red with embarrassment. "That was a rare moment, Alex. I'm normally not so impulsive."

"Too bad," he sighed. He appeared so hopeful. She had to stop gazing into his eyes; she felt like he was about to seduce her again.

***

Back at Dental Connections, Dawn and Lynn were ready to close, but a man was standing in the waiting room.

"I'm sorry, we are closed for the day. Would you like to make an appointment?"

"No, I'm looking for Rosa Fletcher. Can you tell her Yale would like to talk to her?"

"She's not here."

"I see her car parked on the street."

Dawn was wary of giving this man any information. She knew where Rosa was, but threw him off track. "She sometimes stops at the bakery across the street." Dawn and Lynn stood by the office window. They were not going to leave Rosa until they knew what happened. Yale crossed the street and walked into the bakery. When he didn't find her, he headed for the pizzeria. He couldn't believe Rosa was sitting with a different guy, this one tall and blond. She turned when she heard the door open.

"Yale, what are you doing here?"

"I hoped to find you after work. Who is this?"

"Yale, this is Alex, my dance teacher. Alex, this is Yale, a friend from college."

When Alex held out his hand, Yale ignored him. Alex planted a smile on his face and asked, "Would you like a slice?"

Yale was unhappy but composed himself. He didn't see this dance teacher as being a threat. The guy was a fairy.

"Rosa, I wanted to take you out to dinner tonight."

"I'm having dinner now."

Yale was getting frustrated. He planned to take her out for a nice dinner. Instead, she was eating pizza with this loser.

"How about tomorrow?"

"I'm free then, Yale. Mother's Pub is not far from here. I will meet you there at eight so we can talk."

"Fine." Yale looked Alex over with disdain. "Do you normally go out with your students?"

Rosa answered for him. "I'm participating in a ballroom event with Alex. We were discussing the details."

Disinterested and annoyed, Yale swallowed his pride since he had driven from Manhattan to find her sitting with another guy. He tried to be polite. "I'll see you tomorrow, Rosa. Enjoy the pizza."

Rosa was upset when she turned to Alex. "Now you know life is complicated right now. But I would like to learn ballroom and help the Donovans."

"No worries, Rosa. No strings attached; it's just dancing."

They enjoyed the pizza, and Alex insisted she take the rest of the pie home to her roommates.

Chapter 17

Careful thought went into choosing an outfit for dinner with Yale. Rosa did not want to seem provocative, but did not want to appear in business clothes either. She chose a black skirt and a pink Angora sweater. Rosa was getting ready when she heard a soft knock on the door. Chrissy was waiting. She seemed upset.

"I'm sorry, Rosa, are you going out?"

"I am. My ex-boyfriend insisted on taking me to dinner."

"Maybe this isn't a good time to talk."

"I have time, Chrissy. I don't have to meet him until eight." Chrissy had tears in her eyes. "What's wrong?"

"I'm late."

Rosa pondered the statement. "Have you been sick? Sometimes that throws off your cycle."

"No, Rosa, I'm just late."

"Have you discussed it with your boyfriend?"

"He's not my boyfriend anymore. He denied his involvement."

"That's ridiculous."

"He told me he had a vasectomy."

"Liar." Rosa knew the guy was bad news. "Chrissy, I'm sorry, but you have to find out for sure. They sell home pregnancy tests at the drugstore. Should I get one for you?"

"Yes, please."

Rosa hugged her. "Don't panic. There are other circumstances that could cause you to be late."

"Thanks, Rosa. I haven't told anyone else."

"I won't say anything." Rosa had a heavy heart when she drove to Mother's Pub. Her problems were minor compared to what Chrissy was facing. She would purchase the test at the drugstore on the way home.

***

Yale was waiting for her at the restaurant. He looked handsome and seemed relaxed. They talked about their patients and their hopes for the future. He asked Rosa about her roommates and showed genuine interest. He listened as she described dance, an interest they did not share. Yale was practicing with the top cardiac surgeons in the country, a rare opportunity for him to learn and become established. She imagined he would also become an expert in his field. Finally, he talked about their relationship.

"Rosa, I hope you will give it another chance."

She had practiced what she wanted to say, but now she wavered. "I need time. I realize I don't have to worry about what happens next, and I cannot commit to anyone until I find out what I want. Maybe I shouldn't close the door completely, but I can't be your girlfriend.

The timing is not right, and I think our window of opportunity has come and gone."

The hurt was apparent. "I miss you, Rosa."

"I miss you too, Yale. That doesn't mean we belong together."

"When can I see you again?"

"I can't make plans with you since I need my space. I'm here tonight because it ended badly, and I thought we would heal faster if we had an honest conversation about where we stand. I have feelings for you, but it's not enough."

He walked her to her car. She hadn't changed her mind. He admitted it would be difficult to see her because of the demands of his residency program. It would take time and patience to rebuild their bond, and the timing was not right for him either. Rosa wondered how Yale had known her work schedule when he showed up at Dental Connections and suspected her mother had something to do with his sudden appearance. Rosa could no longer tolerate her interference. She returned to a quiet house, so she went to bed.

***

When Rosa woke up, she heard Connie and Chrissy in the kitchen. Chrissy called to her. "Rosa, I have news. I got my period this morning."

"Oh, Chrissy, that's great. I know how worried you were."

"Listen, Rosa, I don't think it was a false alarm. I had terrible cramps last night, and my period is much heavier than usual."

"Should we call your doctor?"

"No, I'm sure I'll be all right."

Rosa was certain Chrissy didn't need a lecture, but she couldn't help herself. "The thing is, Chrissy, they tell us we're liberated and we have a choice, but all of them are heartbreaking. I hope we never have to make that awful decision. I can recommend my doctor, who has been thorough in prescribing the right birth control for me. If careful, it is supposed to be very effective."

Chrissy agreed. "I intend to use a different gynecologist; this one told me my options are limited because of high blood pressure. He never suggested treating my blood pressure, or why I even have high blood pressure. I'm only 22! I don't intend to be sexually active after this. I distrust men, even my gynecologist. But you're right, thank God I didn't have to decide."

Connie prepared breakfast. The girls had a pleasant morning, and Chrissy was thankful for the friendship and support. Rosa put the pregnancy test in the top drawer of her nightstand, hoping that it would remain there, unused.

Chapter 18

The house seemed empty. Nana took her belongings with her when she moved in with Aunt Mary. The walls were bare, and the cabinets removed, and Alex planned to paint before he bought new furniture. The floors, window frames, and moldings were hardwood, and Alex thought a warm white color would complement the woodwork. He drove to the paint store in the morning.

The store was in a strip mall alongside a card store, a coffee shop, and a pet store. Alex had never been to *'Carl's Bird Emporium'*, so he visited before purchasing the paint. The store was noisy and empty except for a large dude sitting at the cash register. Because of his muscular arms, long brown ponytail, and dark glasses, he looked like he should sell motorcycles, not birds. His tattoos looked bold against his pale complexion. At first, he did not acknowledge Alex, then glanced up from his newspaper, startled. He took the earplugs out of his ears. "Can I help you?"

For a moment, Alex forgot what he was going to say. The gentle voice of the owner surprised him. He stared at Carl. "Well, I have a bird, and wondered if or thought maybe he should have a companion."

The hesitation amused Carl. He gave Alex a reassuring smile. "You have come to the right place. Tell me about your pet."

"His name is Buster, and I think he is male, but how can you tell? He is a parakeet with a yellow head, a blue abdomen, and black and white feathers on his back."

"What color is his cere?"

"His what?"

"The skin above his nostrils ... the color above his beak."

"Blue"

"Does your bird sing a lot?"

"He's a real chatterbox."

"Well, you have a male bird then."

"You're kidding. Males sing more than females?"

"They do."

Alex and Carl chuckled, sharing a guy moment. Then Alex continued, "What kind of companion would be appropriate?"

"Parakeets usually get along, so you will probably be successful regardless of which bird you choose. Sometimes when two males cohabitate, they get territorial and have issues, but if you put a female in there, well, you could have eggs. Do you want to breed the parakeets?"

Alex seemed uncomfortable with the thought. "No, but I don't want two males fighting. Are there always eggs?"

"No, in fact, some clients become disappointed when they put a male and female together and nothing happens. Sometimes the pair are just friends. If you do not provide a nesting box, that is often the case."

"It sounds like a female bird without the nesting box might be the right move."

"What is Buster like?"

"He's usually cheerful, but distraught since my grandmother moved out. She was at home all day. Now he is alone while I am at work, and lately, he has been pecking at his mirror and chirping like an alarm clock."

"You have to limit his mirror time. Too much can harm him emotionally."

"Really?"

"Yes, and from what you have told me, I think your bird needs a companion. Would you like to pick one out today?"

"No, I'm not ready yet. It's almost like I am a father arranging a marriage."

Carl looked sideways at Alex and shocked him with his next question. "Do you read romance novels too?"

Alex blushed. He had never admitted that to anyone. He stammered. "They are my grandmother's books; I have only read a few."

Carl's gaze was intense. "This shop is a no-judgment zone; please speak freely."

Alex changed the subject. "What if the birds don't get along?"

"They may be slow to acclimate to each other. If they can't live together, I will take the bird back, as I don't want two birds unhappy or fighting."

"That's fair. I will think about everything you said. Will you be able to show me which birds are female?"

"It's sometimes hard to tell when the birds are young. Color and behavior can normally predict sex, but I have made mistakes. Point out a bird, and I will do my best to get it right."

"Thanks, Carl. I want two birds that are happy together, but I think Buster would prefer a female companion."

Carl tried to give more advice. "Try to think about Buster's personality and what he would want in a companion. Your grandmother was his first companion. Is she quiet, or chatty? Does she sing? Evaluate the way he responds to you. Parakeets interact with their human family the way they interact with other birds."

"I didn't expect to have so much to think about, but if you spend your life in a cage with someone, you should be well-matched."

Carl watched Alex as he left the pet store and hoped he would buy one of his birds. Alex was a nice guy.

***

Alex painted for hours; each time he took a break, he added steps to his waltz. He planned to teach Rosa the waltz number first; her ballet background would make it easy for her to learn. He hoped dancing together would lead them into a relationship. Maybe she would eventually agree to date. Lawrence visited while Alex painted. He helped by playing with Buster and changing his food and water. Lawrence had a big smile when he told Alex about his visit to the dentist. He said she was nice but didn't remember her name. There is no way Alex would forget the name of the dentist who examined him. Fletcher was English, a common name. He thought about her every time he picked up a toothbrush. Maybe that's why he dreamt of her at night.

Chapter 19

Alex taught dance classes on Saturday and met Rosa for choreography in the afternoon. When he played the Viennese Waltz album, they danced without going over the basic steps. He knew she would fall right into the waltz. Alex was a strong lead, and Rosa realized it would be difficult to take a wrong turn; dancing with him was effortless. Her timing was impeccable. He made a few minor adjustments to her frame and told her he would teach her the choreography at the next session. Rosa couldn't wait to see him the following Saturday.

***

Dawn approached Dr. Fletcher after a long and busy Wednesday afternoon. She smiled brightly as she announced, "Dr. Fletcher, your boyfriend is here to see you," then added, "the blond one."

Rosa would talk to Dawn about being so sassy and explain her situation with Yale and Alex. The employees at Dental Connections were still gossiping about the two men who pursued Dr. Fletcher. Rosa was certain the rumors were far more salacious than the reality of the situation. Alex waited in the reception area. He stood up. "I hope you don't mind that I stopped by, but I have shoes for ballroom. You should try to break them in before the next lesson. I can return them if they are uncomfortable." She removed her shoes and socks, and he slipped the dainty heels onto her feet and buckled them for her. Heat flashed through her as she recalled the last time he kneeled before her to unbuckle her shoes, at the foot of his bed. She stood up, and the dance shoes seemed to fit.

"How did you know my size?" she asked.

"I peeked at your street shoes while you were in the studio. The Capezios you wore at our first lesson are proper dance shoes, but high heels and suede soles help to achieve proper ballroom form. I selected two-inch heels; they are easier to dance in."

Rosa admired the silver sandals and wondered if Alex intended to choose her whole outfit. "Will you provide a costume too?"

"I already have one for you. The shoes are new, but the dress is from the dance studio. It is perfect for our purpose: a leotard with different skirts that can easily slip on and off between dances."

Rosa expressed concern. "What if the outfit doesn't fit, or is unattractive on me?"

He evaluated her with a wolfish stare. "I'm sure it will be spectacular on you."

Alex admired the curve of Rosa's figure. She would appear more voluptuous than most other dancers. She was thin, but her long legs and ample bustline gave her sexy appearance. Their height would set them apart. They were stunning as a couple because of their height, and Rosa's sex appeal would project and sell dance lessons for the studio. That served the Donovan's agenda. Alex had his own selfish motive since he could admire her without restraint while teaching her.

***

The rumor at the hospital was that Dr. Ryan and Dr. Fletcher were an item. Gerry was concerned this deception was unfair to Rosa since they were friends, not lovers. They met for dinner one evening after work, and he ordered a bottle of wine as he waited. She wore her work clothes but let down her hair and refreshed her makeup. "Dr. Fletcher, can I interest you in a glass of rose'?" he asked when she approached his table.

"Yes please, Dr. Ryan." They enjoyed teasing each other with formality, and the greeting gave them a thrill.

But he became serious. "Are you aware of the rumors at the hospital? About us?"

"I am Gerry."

"Do you mind?"

"No, Gerry, it's true in a way. I have grown fond of you."

He smiled. "It takes me off the market, so I don't mind. But what about you?"

"I don't care. Who would be discouraged by the impression that we are dating? We work at a geriatric hospital, and the eligible men are over eighty."

"I guess you're right, but other doctors are visiting the facility."

"And most of them are my father's age. I'm not looking for a workplace romance, so this works for me too."

"Are you looking at all, Rosa? Were you hurt by the guy you knew from school? The one at the banquet?"

Rosa sighed, appreciative of Gerry's concern. "I still have a heartache, since I feel like he used me. It was convenient for him when we were both in professional school, and now that he's nearby in New York, he is interested in reconciliation. He didn't want to break up, but he didn't want to commit either. It was unrealistic for him to expect me to follow him without a marriage proposal. I left for the East Coast without him after years of dating."

"Is there anyone else?"

Rosa sighed. "I'm attracted to my dance teacher, but certain nothing will come of it. He has too many women milling about; kind of like you."

"You have me wrong, Rosa. They would be shocked if they knew the truth. I don't see myself as a chick magnet."

"You haven't heard the nurses at the hospital talking about you. Anyway, I am rehearsing with Alex for a performance and see him at the dance school. We are practicing waltz, salsa, and disco numbers. I am worried about the disco."

"Why is that? Disco is so much fun."

"I missed out on disco dancing; I was too busy studying to be a dentist."

"Would you like to go dancing with me?"

" Sure, Gerry. Do you know disco?"

"I do. Are you free this Saturday night? Disco isn't as popular as it used to be, but I know places where we can dance. I can show you what I know. When I revisited dancing at the gala, I realized how much I missed it."

"It's a date. Do you want me to meet you?"

"No, I will pick you up. I'd love to say hi to Connie if she's home."

***

Alex enjoyed the Saturday afternoon dance lesson with Rosa. They finished the waltz choreography and started the salsa. Rosa had to loosen up for Latin dance. He encouraged her to use her hips, shoulders, and other assets.

"I don't know how," she complained.

Alex loosened his shirt, raked his hair back, and showed her what he wanted from her.

"You're a better girl than I am," she laughed.

"I am not. I don't have the right equipment. Maybe you need a drink."

"It's Saturday afternoon."

"And we are alone in the studio. I know where Fred keeps his bottle of scotch."

"Gross."

"Have you ever tried scotch and soda? I'll make you a weak one."

The drink wasn't as bad as she thought it would be. Her inhibitions no longer held her back. She became accustomed to his steamy advances and enjoyed moving with him. It was, after all, just dancing.

***

Alex left the dance studio longing for her and didn't know how he could continue to keep his feelings to himself. He distracted himself with the paint project, but by 10 pm he had paint all over his clothes and was sick of the job. He had to get out of the house. Alex covered Buster, took a quick shower, and headed out. The Blueberry Patch was a disco club frequented by his dance friends. He could always find a dance partner and a cold beer waiting for him. As soon as he entered the establishment, a colleague ushered him onto the dance floor. The woman loved dancing with Alex, and they danced together with ease.

She realized he was distracted when Alex lost his timing. She followed his gaze to Rosa.

"Someone you know, Alex?"

They both looked over at Gerry and Rosa. "Just a friend," he answered.

"Do you want to make her jealous?"

"Not really. I think the normal thing to do is to continue the dance."

He had never felt so insecure. He ordered a beer and headed to their table. It would be best to say hello to Rosa and her date and get it over with.

"Hi, Rosa. I see you are getting prepared for the disco choreography. You already know the basics." He looked at Gerry and offered his hand. "I'm Alex, the dance teacher."

"Hi Alex. Gerry Ryan. I work with Rosa at the hospital."

The two shook hands. Alex tried to be friendly but didn't want to linger or intrude on their date. But Gerry made a surprising suggestion. "You should go over some steps right now. Rosa still wants to dance, but I need a break."

Rosa, embarrassed, went along with the suggestion. She took Alex's hand and led him to the dance floor. He repeated the steps Gerry taught her and easily fell into a rhythm with her. Alex felt guilty as he allowed the dance to become personal and intimate. He knew she was on a date, but couldn't help himself. Reluctantly, he let her go. "You're a wonderful dancer, Rosa. Sorry to intrude on your date."

"Gerry doesn't mind, and now I have a greater understanding of how the dance is supposed to feel."

When Rosa returned to the table, Gerry took Rosa's hand. "You looked awesome together."

"I'm glad since we perform in less than two months."

"Be honest, Rosa, it's not just dancing."

"What makes you say that?"

"Open your eyes. The guy looked devastated when he saw you here with me, though he tried to be a good sport."

"Alex and I are not dating, so I'm sure you're wrong. Alex can have any woman he wants. He was just surprised to see me dancing before the lesson."

"Believe me, Rosa, he wants you. I like him and did not sense any red flags from our brief encounter. The other guy seems more of a philanderer than this one."

"You mean Yale?"

"Yes, my gut tells me you shouldn't trust him."

Gerry didn't tell her about the conversation with his friend from New York, Dr. Patel, who complained about Yale's reputation among the nurses. Dr. Patel described him as a talented resident but hoped he would settle down as he got older. Yale's indiscretions had become a common topic of hospital gossip. As a friend, Gerry tried to steer her away from thoughts of reconciliation with Yale. When Gerry and Rosa left the Blueberry Patch, she thought about what Gerry had said and how Alex had made her feel on the dance floor. She found it hard to believe her dance teacher was interested. After all, his exact words were, '*No strings attached; it's only dancing.*'

Chapter 20

Carl did most of his business on the weekends, but the sales were usually pet food and accessories. When Alex entered the store, he expected to sell him a bird. He was busy assisting another customer but waved to Alex to assure him he would be with him in a few minutes. Carl was always happy when he found a home for one of his parakeets. He gave Alex time to shop. Alex had his eye on one, a beauty, white with aqua-blue patches of color on her tummy. Carl finally made his way over to Alex. "Do you have questions?"

He pointed to the little white bird. "Is that one a female?"

"I'm pretty sure she is. She has been here for a few months, and her cere has remained pink. Though beautiful, I must warn you that other clients have decided not to buy her. She is quiet and unsociable."

"Is that unusual?"

"Maybe quiet was not the right word. She is silent. I have never heard a peep out of her."

"Do you think it's a medical problem?"

"Could be. Maybe she is deaf, maybe something's wrong with her vocal cords, or perhaps she is just antisocial. She's a loner. She seems content to perch quietly by herself."

Alex felt compassion for this lonely creature. "Do you think she would like a companion?"

"I'm sure she would prefer one companion to many. Look at how many parakeets are in the cage with her."

Alex, deep in thought, looked to Carl for a final question.

"Do you think she could have babies?"

"I don't know, but most parakeets attract verbally, so it's unlikely."

"I'll take her."

Carl left for the back room and brought out a small birdcage. "You can use this for travel and to keep her in her own space; put the cage next to Buster's. After a week, put her in with him."

Alex watched as Carl opened the large group cage and picked up the little bird. She gazed at him and didn't resist.

"I don't think I can pick her up like that," warned Alex.

"Would you like me to help you next week?"

"You would do that?"

"Do you have beer?"

"I do."

"Could you tell me what night works best for you? On weekdays I close at 7. If you have the beer, I will bring the pizza."

When Alex gave his address, they realized they were neighbors. Carl owned a home two blocks from Alex. He also had an upstairs tenant. They already had a few interests in common: the neighborhood, parakeets, and beer. Alex named the little white bird Cleopatra, Cleo for short. Both birds stared at each other throughout the week. Alex wondered if this was abnormal.

***

Lawrence begged his mother to allow him to join the guys the night Cleopatra moved in with Buster. Tammy made Alex promise to send him back upstairs by 8:30 or sooner if he was being a pest. Alex wondered if Lawrence would be shy around Carl, who looked intimidating. When Carl arrived with the pizza, Lawrence was all smiles. Carl knew to say the right thing. "Al, who's your friend? You didn't tell me this would be a night out with the guys."

"This is my buddy Lawrence."

"Nice to meet you, Lawrence." Carl's friendly voice softened his tough exterior, and Lawrence was anxious to be his friend. Alex served Lawrence ginger ale with a cherry, a treat since Tammy rarely had a soda in the house. They told silly jokes and enjoyed the pizza. Then, Carl facilitated the move. It seemed underwhelming. Carl moved Cleo into the cage with Buster, and they stared at each other and froze; no sound, no movement.

"Is this normal?" asked Alex.

"Give it time, Al; at least they are aware. Sometimes birds coexist and ignore their roommates."

Then Lawrence started asking difficult questions. "Is Cleo Buster's girlfriend?"

Alex answered. "I guess so, Lawrence."

"That's nice," he replied. "Alex likes a girl, but he's not sure she likes him."

Alex rolled his eyes. No secrets were safe around Lawrence. But Carl was amused and softened the moment. "Lawrence, I would like to have a girlfriend too."

"My mom's a girl," he said with enthusiasm.

Carl hesitated. "Well, maybe I could meet her sometime."

The clock saved Carl from further inquiry. Lawrence scuttled up the stairs at 8:35. The thought of Carl and Tammy together seemed ridiculous to Alex. Carl was nice but weird, and he spoke without filters. Because of his large build and tattoos that covered his bulky arms, he appeared ominous, but his voice was gentle. He was confident and cool-headed, but unshaven and sloppy, and his t-shirts were from the 70s. At least he had the courtesy to leave his 'disco sucks' shirt in the drawer. Tammy, in contrast, had impeccable taste. She was businesslike and always said the right thing. If they dated, it would be an interracial relationship; that was uncommon and not widely accepted. Alex couldn't see them as a couple, but was sure they would meet and wondered what that would be like. Because he was a dance teacher, Alex didn't have many guy friends and was happy to have beer and conversation with Carl, who was philosophical and comfortable being himself. He invited Carl over the following week for the camaraderie and to monitor the birds.

Chapter 21

It all started on Monday at Dental Connections. Rosa was trying a crown on a patient's second molar. The patient was full of saliva, and Dawn tried to help, resulting in a mishap when the crown disappeared into the suction by mistake. It happened in an instant. Dawn realized what she had done, shocked by her clumsiness. Rosa needed a moment to think as she sat the patient up to rinse. She didn't know what to say.

"Mr. Miller, I don't know how to tell you this, but we just suctioned up your new crown."

"I know," he replied.

"We should be able to retrieve and sterilize it. In the worst-case scenario, we will return the model to the lab so they can fabricate another crown."

"I understand, Dr. Fletcher."

This is how Rosa's week started. Patient confessions characterized the rest of the week.

"I'm sorry, but I didn't floss."

"The temporary came out, but I forgot it was there when I chewed that gummy bear."

"My bonding chipped, but I hold hairpins in my mouth."

"I ate a Tootsie Roll last night, then my filling came out."

"I'm so tired at college. I usually forget to brush my teeth."

That last one disturbed Dr. Fletcher. She treated many students who left for college with virgin teeth, only to return during the break with cavities. The patients sometimes blurted out, "*I know you're going to yell at me,*" but she never yelled at a patient. The patient's responsibility was to follow her recommendations. If they did not, her job was to control the damage. She did not judge, but was honest about the condition of their teeth. Rosa always commented on improvements. Encouragement helped.

***

When Rosa confessed to Dawn that she had spent the night with Alex, she didn't expect to have another conversation about it. Dawn witnessed the body language between Rosa and Alex when he slipped the ballroom shoes on in the waiting room. It reminded Dawn of Cinderella and Prince Charming. Of course, the slipper would fit, and happiness was within Rosa's reach if only she would stop resisting. Dr. Fletcher needed to seize the moment and take it. Rosa did not have self-confidence, and Dawn wished she could convince her boss that she needed to relax and take Alex's attention more seriously.

With two dances behind them, Alex concentrated on disco. This was the most challenging routine. It was fast-paced, with lifts and intoxicating choreography. Rosa felt flushed from the physical exertion and the emotional roller coaster she felt when so close to him. The magnetism was exhausting, and it seemed like dancing did not go far enough to satisfy her. They practiced without music for several weeks, and Rosa wondered if he had trouble deciding on a song. Finally, she asked about it. "Alex, I feel uncomfortable not knowing the music. Why haven't you told me?"

"The choreography is difficult, and a common teaching method is to learn the dance before putting it to music. Besides, I wasn't sure you would like the song. It's too late to change now. The choreography is perfect with this music."

He found the album and put it on, Donna Summer's *'I Feel Love'.* The dance was fast, building, and progressively more intimate. At the end he dipped her into a submissive pose, their lips close but never touching. She was flushed and embarrassed by the way the dance affected her. She stepped away from him and folded her arms over her chest. "What are you trying to sell, Alex?"

"Dance lessons," he said innocently.

Rosa could not hide what she was feeling. "It felt like foreplay."

"You are too sensitive, Rosa, but I understand you are not a professional dancer. I was afraid you would think the number suggestive, but the dance is all about emotion. I'm sure the audience will relate to this dance in particular."

She had to admit the steps were not inappropriate. The overall feeling, the progression, and the intensity as they drew closer made it intimate and dangerous. The audience would see them as lovers, at first hesitant but soon captured and unable to resist the unmistakable attraction they felt. Her surrender was in the final pose. The choreography was brilliant, but too close to reality for Rosa. She assumed she was overreacting because of her amateur status and because she could not distance her personal emotions from the dance. Rosa imagined it didn't look as provocative as it felt. Besides, the performance would be in front of strangers, except for Chrissy, who would act as her stage mom, and Gerry if he decided to attend.

Jackie brought the costume out, and Rosa tried it on. The bodice's neckline was plunging, and the leotard had a low back. The long-sleeved costume was adorned with silver sequins that sparkled like diamonds. Alex admired the fit. "You are stunning. This costume looks spectacular on you."

"I never danced in anything so revealing."

"You will have a sheer jacket and a long flowing skirt for the waltz," said Jackie. "Even with the short skirt, it is more conservative than most of the ballroom outfits. Sometimes the women have on less than a bathing suit."

Rosa knew Jackie was right, but could not believe how sexy she looked. She recalled how Patrick and Alex had ogled her the night she wore her black dress. And she remembered how that evening had ended.

Chapter 22

Alex stopped by the Madison Hotel to evaluate the venue for the ballroom event. He was familiar with the dance floor since he had already performed there. When he grabbed a program to determine how much time they had between dances, he discovered his salsa number was after a professional couple using the same song. The audience could not help comparing the performances since both dances were salsa, and the music was the same. Alex wasn't sure how he could fix this. As he drove by Donovan's dance studio, he thought he might get advice from Jackie or Fred. He knocked first, then used his key, and found that Fred was sitting in the business office.

"Alex, shouldn't you rest before your busy day? I assume you will work all day and perform in the evening."

"I will sleep after I make a decision. JD Dance Studio has a salsa right before ours; it is the same song and probably the same version. I don't want to follow them. Should I ask them to move our dance?"

"What is the salsa choreography like, Al?"

"It's basic with some razzle-dazzle. Because Rosa is a beginner, I choreographed only one dance difficult enough for competition, and that one is disco."

"Why not substitute the song? Salsa is a feeling often expressed without specific choreography. I suspect the best salsa dancers are on the streets of Havana right now, without planned choreography."

"You have a point, Fred. I have tried to teach Rosa to feel the steps rather than memorize them. She has become like an athlete who psyches herself into the zone. But what song?"

"I know a song perfect for Rosalinda, if it works with the choreography."

" Which one? I need a song she would be comfortable with."

"*Rosalinda's Eyes.*"

"You mean the Billy Joel song? Fred, you are brilliant. I am sure she knows it. I am going to try it and make sure the choreography fits."

"Listen, Alex, I taught Rosa as a little girl, and even then she was a perfectionist who liked to be prepared. If I were you, I wouldn't give her too much time to worry about the change."

"I hate to be deceptive, but perhaps you're right. This song is a good choice for her. It doesn't require her to appear sultry and seductive; it is more about love, and the instrumentals have a cheerful vibe."

When Alex thought about Rosalinda at the ranch, and how she captured him with the brilliance of her beautiful eyes, he became emotional. The song was perfect, and he wondered why he hadn't thought of it. Fred's mundane superpower was to put a student and a song together in a matter of seconds.

***

Alex drove Rosa and Chrissy to the Madison Hotel. Chrissy applied Rosa's makeup, styled her hair and helped with her costume. The hotel lobby housed prospective students and professional dancers, but Rosa and Chrissy were the two women who turned heads as they entered the ballroom. Rosa looked like a glamorous actress, and Chrissy was always stunning, even though she dressed for comfort in her T-shirt and jeans. Alex only had eyes for Rosa but had to chuckle when he saw Chrissy take a seat in the audience next to Russ. He hoped his cousin would remember to breathe.

Alex gave Rosa a pep talk before the waltz. "You can do this dance in your sleep," he started. "It's simple and elegant and meant to impress the engaged couples who imagine a wedding dance for themselves. Think of me as a groom sharing the first dance with his new bride."

Rosa could not believe he had said that. Alex had a talent for promoting fantasy and evoking deep emotions. The image of Alex as her handsome groom is a luxury she would allow herself for the next three minutes. After that, she would return to reality. Alex was a smart businessman. The other studios presented their best professional talent, but Alex chose a partner and a performance that this audience could relate to. The crowd loved the simple, elegant dance.

Rosa removed the sheer jacket and changed her skirt for the salsa. Alex had not warned her about the new song. The other couple doing salsa were walking onto the dance floor. Alex put his arm around her. "Rosa, do you trust me?"

"Of course, Alex. Is something wrong?"

"Will you follow me and submit yourself to me?"

Now she was getting apprehensive. "I guess so."

"I had to change the song for our salsa. The couple from JD Dance chose the song we used in practice."

"You tell me this now?"

"I only found out last night. I didn't want you to be anxious because of the change. The dance doesn't have to be perfect. The performance will be good if you follow me and don't think."

She tried to calm herself; this was more excitement than she could endure. She watched the other couple and understood why Alex had to change the song.

"What song?"

He ignored the question. "Looks like we're up. You know the song. It is about love and longing and being together. You will feel the vibe immediately." He took her hand and led her to the center of the ballroom. He raised her hand to his lips and kissed her wrist.

Oh my God, she thought. *Why did he have to do that?* Afterward, her mind went blank, still flustered by the kiss. When she heard '*Rosalinda's Eyes*' she got emotional. Suddenly there was no one in the room but Alex. When she looked into his eyes, she knew he was emotional too. The result was unrehearsed, inherent and from the heart, moving and brilliant. They were breathless as they finished the dance, barely hearing the overwhelming applause.

"Thank you, Alex; that was touching."

" I'm proud of you, Rosa. That was a leap of faith that we took together. We should unwind for a few minutes. Here comes Chrissy to help you with the disco skirt."

Chrissy was all smiles. "Your first two dances were marvelous. '*Rosalinda's Eyes*' was so moving, I felt like kissing the cute guy sitting next to me."

"That's Russ, Alex's cousin."

"Oh, how exciting! Perhaps I should introduce myself."

Rosa wondered why their disco was the last dance of the evening. Then she saw the disco ball hanging from the ceiling. If they added lighting, it would serve as a finale. The costume was perfect, with the silver sequins shimmering in the soft light. Alex noticed Yale in the audience and realized he should distract Rosa from looking at the crowd. He had one more pep talk.

"It's just you and me out there, and we do not need to engage the audience during this dance. It is intimate, just between us. Just look at me, trust me, and surrender to the dance."

Rosa's head began to spin, and she couldn't think. The lights dimmed, the disco ball activated, and a spotlight illuminated them. She couldn't see the audience if she wanted to. Rosa clung to Alex as he guided her through the dance. It was a blur, but she didn't miss a beat. When he posed with her at the end, their lips nearly touching, the longing was raw and intense. For a moment, the audience was silent. Russ looked at Chrissy, and she gave him a look that made him wish he had a room. The sexual energy was intense. Then applause, a standing ovation, and a crowd gathered around them.

Rosa was relieved the performance was over, but felt exposed. She was not acting during the dances and was certain the audience knew they had been lovers. She was happy to see Russ and Chrissy but somehow embarrassed when confronted by Gerry and his partner Art. They all raved about the performance. Then, her parents surprised her.

"Dad, Mom, what are you doing here?"

"We heard about the performance and decided to come," replied Anita. "Why didn't you invite us?"

Alex looked pale. "Mr. Fletcher?"

"You're dancing with my daughter, Alex."

Rosa was confused. "You two know each other?"

"Alex is the tax preparer I hired to take over Grandpa Diaz's accounts. I didn't know you were dating."

"We're not," they replied in unison.

When Alex met Rosa Fletcher, he realized she shared the same last name as his boss but couldn't imagine that the meek, mild-mannered accountant could be her father. She was at least three inches taller and didn't look like him. Fletcher was such a common name. It was just another bad luck story to have her protective father sitting in the audience..

Anita wanted to know what was going on. She looked at Gerry. "Who are you?"

"I'm a physician at the hospital. I work with Rosa."

Anita then looked at Art. "I'm with him," he mumbled.

Then she looked at Alex. She was astonished. "You're the Mouse King, the fairy."

Rosa followed her mother's gaze to the chairs in the audience; most spectators had left or were inquiring about lessons in the lobby. Yale was sitting there alone, not knowing what to do. It was all too much for Rosa to comprehend. She ran to the parking lot in tears. Yale followed. He was upset. Mrs. Fletcher told him Rosa was not dating anyone, and he wanted to show support by attending her performance. But she already had two men there for her, Dr. Ryan, who Yale thought an idiot not to recognize the sparks between Rosa and Alex, and Alex, who was generating sparks so intense it made the audience feel hot. Yale wasn't ready to give up on Rosa and controlled his anger.

"Rosa, I'm sorry. I thought it would be a way to show support for your dancing. I guess it wasn't a good idea to come."

"No, it wasn't. I didn't want my friends and relatives at this performance. How did you know about it?"

Yale shrugged his shoulders. He didn't want to say. Rosa knew her mother had to be behind it, but wondered how she had found out. "I don't want to talk about this, Yale."

"Where is your car?" he asked.

"Chrissy and I drove with Alex, but for a moment, I was upset and forgot I didn't have my car. I ran out only to remember it wasn't here."

"Can I drive you and Chrissy back?"

"Ok."

Yale and Rosa returned to the building. Alex watched them from the lobby and knew Rosa was angry. When she approached him, he tried to appease her. "I'm sorry, Rosa, I didn't mean for any of this to happen."

"Did you know about my parents and Yale?"

"I noticed Yale in the audience after the salsa number. Otherwise, I had no idea he would be here, and I didn't expect your parents. I'll get your jacket and drive you and Chrissy home."

"Never mind, we have a ride." She then took her frustration out on him. "You know, Alex, you got the performance you wanted out of me. I hope you're satisfied."

He was sorry and hurt; his intention was never to embarrass her in front of her parents. It was not a good way to reveal their relationship to the world, and she did not want to admit there was a relationship. She needed time to calm down.

"I don't blame you for everything that happened, Alex, but some of it was your fault. I didn't think my family would be here to witness that dance. I can't believe my father saw us during that provocative last number. How do you think he feels? I was out of my comfort zone; you knew it and led me there anyway."

"That was never my intention. I wanted to get close to you, and that is the only way you would allow it. I'm so very sorry."

"We will talk again, but I need some space. I don't think I can discuss this now. I feel used."

That was an unfair characterization, but Alex remained silent. He expressed himself through dance and didn't think he had done anything wrong. Now all he could do was wait and see if he still had a chance.

Chapter 23

Alex dreaded a confrontation with Oliver Fletcher the next morning. Oliver was angry. Alex arrived early and braced himself for a stern talk. He was called into Mr. Fletcher's office.

"Sit down, Alex. This is personal, not business."

"Yes, sir."

Oliver paused and stared for a minute or two. The effect was intimidating. He sighed and chose his words. "I know entertainers are all liberal and creative, but I am not. The dance with my daughter was inappropriate, and I'm no fool. It is not just dancing. So my question is, what are your intentions and how will they affect my daughter?"

Alex tried to collect his thoughts. Oliver was direct but fair, and they had worked as a team for many months. Alex revealed something to Oliver that, up to that point, he hadn't yet admitted to himself. "I am interested in a serious relationship with Rosa. I hope she will commit to me."

The answer surprised Oliver. He didn't think Alex was dating his daughter. He maintained a stern look but was relieved. "Well, how is it going?"

"Not well, sir."

Oliver gave Alex some advice. "Rosa is a sweet girl who has allowed herself to be bullied by friends and relatives with forceful personalities. My wife has tried to relive her life through Rosa, and that has been harmful to our daughter's self-esteem. Rosa must find her way, and because of her timid nature, I fear a relationship with a man could dominate and stifle her. I want her happily married to someone who will not take advantage of her. Do you understand what I am saying?"

"Yes, sir. I would never intentionally hurt Rosa or try to control her."

"I like you, Alex, but love Rosa more than anything. I do not want her to be hurt or abandoned. I assume you have engaged in risky behavior, and I am concerned. She is an adult, and I should trust her judgment, but must warn you I own a shotgun."

"You won't have to use it on me, Mr. Fletcher. If you want, I will promise to be a perfect gentleman."

Oliver knew Alex well enough to realize that he would not keep that promise. "What I want is assurance that you won't say something you don't mean. She's fragile."

"I can promise, Mr. Fletcher."

Oliver had planned a different conversation, but now it was irrelevant. He did not know how Rosa felt, but believed Alex had serious intentions. These two young people would make mistakes, and Oliver was not sure Alex was a good match for her, but he did not want to interfere with their personal lives. He tried to reassure Alex.

"As far as I am concerned, the topic is closed. We have work to do, and I need you at the office. But I want Rosa to be treated with respect and do not want a reason to interfere as a protective father in the future. Do I make myself clear?"

"Yes, Mr. Fletcher." Alex headed toward the door but did not leave before hearing one final thought.

"And Alex"

"Yes?"

"I never did like Yale."

Alex smiled. "Neither did I."

***

Alex returned home after a long day at work, physically and emotionally exhausted. He made a sandwich for himself and watched the birds. Buster was singing; he showed off by bobbing his head and wagging his tail. He approached Cleopatra and caressed the side of her head. She did not reciprocate, but Buster did not seem frustrated by her failure to respond and did not give up. Carl would be over in a few days, so Alex planned to ask about the birds and thought he could confide in Carl about how he messed up his relationship with Rosa. Carl was thoughtful and philosophical.

When Alex did not hear from Rosa, he sent flowers to Dental Connections, hoping for a response from her. Everyone at work admired the flowers; she told them they were from her dance teacher. Dawn collected copies of the local paper because it had an article about the ballroom event and a picture of Rosa and Alex in the last moments of their disco dance. It could have been the cover of a romance novel: Alex so tall and handsome, and Rosa in his arms in what appeared to be surrender. Dawn continued to ask Rosa about Alex; she was concerned that Dr. Fletcher did not have enough confidence to recognize that the guy was crazy about her.

Rosa waited until the following Saturday to return her costume from the showcase. She hoped to speak to Alex. Jackie was at the front desk and greeted Rosa with a smile.

"The performance was an enormous success. We may have to hire additional instructors because of the number of students interested."

"I'm glad, Jackie. I am returning the leotard and would like to talk to Alex if he is available."

"His class will end in fifteen minutes. Please stay. He has been waiting for you, and I think I should talk to you myself."

"Sure, Miss Jackie."

They walked into the business office, and Jackie shut the door. "I appreciate how hard you worked on the dances, and I am sorry the evening ended before I could properly thank you. I'm afraid I am the guilty party who told your mother about the performance. I met her at the mall and assumed your parents would attend. When I mentioned the Madison Hotel, I realized you had not told her about the showcase, but I had already revealed too much information to take it back. I had no idea you hadn't told them."

"It's fine, Jackie. How would you know I didn't invite them to the performance?"

Jackie sighed. "I feel responsible for the hard feelings between you and Alex. You must understand his intent was not to get a performance out of you. It was a favor to me and the studio. He had nothing to gain."

"I understand."

"Alex is a brilliant choreographer, but when he is also the performer, he allows his emotions to become part of the dance. I suspect he used the showcase as an excuse to spend time with you."

Rosa was skeptical. Jackie thought she should talk to her about Alex since he rarely talked about himself. She wanted Rosa to know the challenges Alex faced growing up. "Do you know anything about his family?" she asked.

"No, he never talks about himself."

"Fred and I are close to Alex but not related. We were friends with his Nana and with his grandfather. Alex grew up with his grandparents, but was especially close to his grandfather. Grandpa was a Cub Scout leader, and they enjoyed fishing and working in the garden, and were always in the driveway playing basketball. Alex was only nine years old when Grandpa died of a heart attack; it was sudden and tragic. That's when Fred and I, who were like a surrogate aunt and uncle, brought him to the studio. Fred taught him tap, which he immediately liked and excelled at. Little girls surrounded Alex, and his good-natured teasing made him a popular student in the dance school. When he applied to colleges, I encouraged him to try for a dance scholarship. He was a talented basketball player in high school, but I knew the local college offered a full ride for dance and thought he would get it. Nana had struggled with finances, and I knew they couldn't afford college without the scholarship. That is how he ended up dancing professionally. He double-majored in accounting and dance."

The story was touching. Now Rosa remembered dancing with him at the ranch had been divine. He was a natural, but at the time he had not considered a future in dance.

"Alex never mentioned any of this. Do you think he would eventually talk to me about it?"

"I have never heard him speak of his past, but I know he holds it close to his heart. He finds it difficult to express his feelings. He's a good man. I don't know if he's what you are looking for, but the woman he ends up with will be getting a prince."

Just then, Alex opened the door of the office. Jackie and Rosa looked up, immediately silenced.

"Were you talking about me?"

Jackie smirked. "Why do men always think they are the topic of conversation? Give me a break."

"Sorry, Jackie. Rosa, do you have a minute?"

Rosa stood up and followed him into the studio. He didn't know what to say, so he waited. She didn't know what to say, so she watched him silently as he walked to the turntable with the Donna Summer album. He started the music, held out his hand. There was no audience. The closeness and passion were unmistakable as they moved together. When he released her from the final pose, they talked. Rosa took the lead.

"We need a step back, Alex. When we were teenagers, we knew how to start a relationship, but now it seems we don't have a clue. I am confused by the nights together, the dancing, the times we have been together but avoided dating each other. All the crazy coincidences have brought us together and, at the same time, something has kept us apart. It is time to be honest. What do you want to do?"

"Would you like to go out with me, Rosa? Or would you like to become friends at the dance school? Or maybe you'd like to come over and see my painting."

"I didn't know you were a painter."

"Honestly, a wall painter."

"I'm glad you have decided to be honest."

Alex knew the time was right to stop kidding around. "I want to start over if you are willing. We have so much in common, and I enjoy dancing with you. I can only hope that you will someday want more."

"We are having a barbecue at the house tonight. Connie and Charlie are preparing everything, and Chrissy will be home. Charlie might like to have another guy there. Do you want to come over?"

"Sure. What's Charlie like?"

"He's fun, likes to drink beer, and dates Connie. He likes to bowl."

"Sounds like Russ, except for dating Connie, of course. I'll be there."

"See you at 7."

Chapter 24

Charlie and Alex had a beer in hand, a masculine way to start a conversation. They were outside manning the grill while Rosa, Connie, and Chrissy prepared side dishes and desserts in the kitchen. The hamburgers and hotdogs were almost ready. Charlie flipped the burgers and turned to Alex. " I heard about the drama at that dance show. It was the topic of conversation all week."

"I'm not sure what version of that story you heard, Charlie. I choreographed a dance that some would consider risque. Rosa's parents, boss, and ex-boyfriend were in the audience. Rosa was stunning in the dance, but she was uncomfortable with the steamy choreography. It embarrassed her when she realized her parents were in attendance."

"Well, it was just a dance, right?"

"That's the thing, Charlie. It was more than a dance; it felt like a prelude to, well, you know. I wasn't thinking with my intellect when I choreographed it."

"Has anything happened between you and Rosa?"

Alex looked down. The answer was obvious. "Well," noted Charlie, "she seems to be over it now. What did you do?"

"I don't have a clue."

They told tales over a bonfire and toasted marshmallows. Alex had interesting stories about his dance career, but the most memorable ones happened as a child. He reminisced.

"My first recital was a turning point when I realized I could perform. I was supposed to dance in one group number but was backstage during the entire show as a helper to Fred. The finale was a party scene, and a little girl was going to jump out of a cake. When they rolled the cake onto the stage, the girl was nowhere to be found. In a desperate moment, Fred told me to get into the cake. He told me to jump out when I felt three taps on the side of the prop. While I sat inside that cake, I heard the girl crying backstage. She missed her big moment. When I felt the cue, I jumped out, and my movements were hilarious since I didn't know the dance. I looked ridiculous, unrehearsed, and comical, but it was what everyone talked about weeks later. My affinity for comedy continues; I heard plenty of laughter when I was in The Nutcracker."

Chrissy, Connie, and Rosa heard the end of the conversation as they walked onto the patio.

Connie asked, "What part did you play?"

"Mouse King and Sugarplum Fairy."

The image was ridiculous. Rosa had to smile since she saw it firsthand. The night was full of humor, and Charlie was more animated because of his camaraderie with Alex. Both men had fun entertaining the girls. When Rosa walked Alex to his car, she kissed his cheek and agreed to go out with him again. They made plans for the following weekend.

***

During the week, Carl walked over to Alex's place to discuss Buster and Cleo. Carl prepared chicken parmesan in Alex's kitchen; he was a talented chef, another surprise. They set the table for four. Lawrence bounded into the room. "Mommy will be down in a few minutes. She's bringing a salad."

Carl straightened his posture and took notice when Tammy entered the room. He was not handsome, but he had an attractive smile that softened his looks. He took Tammy's hand and raised his eyebrows. "Lawrence told me you were a girl, but he didn't mention you were such a beautiful one."

"I am quite pleased to see you, Carl."

He kissed the back of her hand. "I have been a fool, and right now I feel foolish."

"How so?"

"Because the script seems to be out of my grasp. Some men are born great, some achieve greatness, and some have greatness thrown upon them."

Alex looked at them, not comprehending the odd conversation. Then Tammy giggled. "Carl and I went to the same high school. We met each other while performing '*Twelfth Night*'. I was Maria, and Carl was the fool."

"Of course he was," added Alex.

Carl continued to admire Tammy. "I tried to remember an appropriate line from the play, but that is the only one I could think of."

"You were at Mommy's school?" asked Lawrence.

Alex was living in a world of coincidences. Tammy and Carl were high school friends; Carl, a senior, and Tammy, a freshman. There seemed to be a spark between them that was ready to ignite. They had a lively evening because of this reunion, and Lawrence was excited about Carl meeting his mom. At 9 o'clock, Lawrence and Tammy said goodnight and went upstairs. Alex brought up the subject of his pets, as he expected Cleo would be more of a companion to Buster.

"Is it normal for her to act so distant?"

"Not really," said Carl. "By now there should be verbal communication or reciprocation when he tries to groom her. She exhibited the same behavior when at the shop. Parakeets are supposed to be social."

"Can I help?" asked Alex.

"There is one thing you can do, but I'm not sure you will think it is a good idea. If you put a birdbath in the cage, and she sees Buster in it, she may want to join him. But sometimes being in the water together encourages them to mate."

"I doubt that would happen," replied Alex. "She doesn't seem interested in him at all."

"I'm not so sure," said Carl. "By the way, does Tammy have a boyfriend?"

Chapter 25

Thoughts of spending time at the beach with Alex occupied her thoughts all week. When Rosa was a teenager, she dreamed of a beach date with a handsome boy. It never happened. Yale was her only boyfriend. They lived in the Midwest, and she wasn't sure if he enjoyed the beach. She was twenty-six years old and finally, her dream was about to come true. Better late than never. Rosa loved to play in the water. The ocean would be cold in June, but Rosa didn't care and hoped Alex would enjoy the waves as much as she did. Her one-piece bathing suit was sexy but secure. The crashing surf could claim many items: bathing suit tops, jewelry, and even dentures. Rosa had treated a patient who had lost his swimming at the Jersey shore.

Alex picked her up early on Saturday morning so they could avoid traffic. The day was perfect: clear, warm, and in the low 80s. They listened to cassettes, talked, and sang, and in no time they were at the beach on a glorious morning. They were ready for an active day. Rosa brought sandwiches and snacks, and Alex packed the cooler with beverages. They planned to stay all day, and since it was high tide, they settled near the water.

Rosa shed her shorts and shirt and headed for the ocean. Alex followed. After seeing her in that bathing suit, he would have followed her anywhere. The sea was numbing, but the excitement of the day and the joy of being together warmed them enough to get acclimated to the conditions. They were strong swimmers, but the ocean was rough with an undertow, so they were aware of each other and stayed close. When Rosa wiped out in a wave, Alex was there to rescue her. Alex was constantly wiping out, so she would have to rescue him. Afterward, he would thank her with a dashing smile and a spontaneous hug. His adolescent ploys were funny and an excuse for her to grab onto him. Rosa let him have his fun; after all, she had lured him into the sea, and she expected the teasing and touching since they had always been physical. But the gnawing restlessness she felt was a shock to her. It felt primitive sharing the surf and lying next to him on the beach blanket as they dried off. She tried to avoid these thoughts, though it was difficult to block out the memories of dancing together and of that passionate night of lovemaking. As they warmed in the afternoon sun, they held hands and talked, discovering how much they had in common. They were athletic, liked the same music, and loved water sports. The ocean was their playground.

"You were very shy when I met you at the ranch," Alex noted. "We barely spoke the entire week."

"I thought you were just being nice because it was your job," Rosa revealed. "I didn't want to monopolize your time."

"It started as a job, but in time I became interested in you, Rosa. We seemed to get along."

"I haven't seen Angelica for years," she admitted, "but I am glad she brought me on her trip. It was an amazing vacation because I overcame my fear of riding horses and learned that I didn't need Angelica to feel grown up. I also enjoyed my first kiss."

"I was your first?"

"You were."

"I'm glad, Rosa, since I remember it as being amazing. How old were you?"

"Sixteen. I was a late bloomer, and pretty inexperienced. I wanted to wait until it meant something. It did."

He held her hand even tighter and sensed this was meant to be. After his many wrong turns, he rediscovered a longing felt in his youth.

"I was a late bloomer too, Rosa, a nerd in school, though I played basketball."

"So did I. I will have to challenge you to a game of one on one."

" I'm sure you will win. If I play with you, I will probably foul out."

After kissing and hand-holding, they once again plunged into the water. The spectacular June day ended too soon. The lifeguards were done with their shift, the families with children were long gone, and the beach was nearly empty. Rosa felt like she could stay there forever. The air was clean and salty, the sound of the waves mesmerizing, and the vastness of the ocean had a calming effect. They savored the day and the time they spent together, and sat in a breathless silence. Finally, they packed up their belongings and headed out to the car. Alex didn't know he had made her fantasy come true. He brought her home and kissed her goodnight; it was gentle, sweet, and full of promise. It felt right, and her heart told her to give Alex a chance.

Alex loved the beach, but being there with Rosa was special. He finally found someone who wanted to stay in the water with him. Although tired and full of sand, he felt content. He was anxious to shower and knew he would sleep soundly. As he entered the house, he heard noises from the kitchen; he recognized Buster's happy sound, but there was a different voice, a soft chirping. Cleo. They were in the water together, splashing and playing. He remembered what Carl had said about the birdbath, but didn't have the heart to take it out of the cage. After a few minutes they perched together, and Alex placed the blanket over their cage. Alex retired to his comfortable bed and fell asleep, dreaming of Rosa. He wondered, was the chemistry they felt enough to bring them together?

Chapter 26

A gentle breeze whispered across the lake, and the backyard umbrellas were on display. The gathering was small: Rosa, her parents, Grandpa Diaz, and the neighbors across the street, Shane and Rita Murphy. Anita insisted on having a party for Rosa's 27th birthday. Being 27 meant she was in her late 20s and life would soon change. Her friends from college were getting married and having children, and Rosa planned to follow suit in the next few years. She wanted a husband and a family, and though her career was important, she knew it was not enough to fulfill her.

She missed Shane and Rita, who had been a part of her life growing up. Shane had recent health problems that required frequent visits to his physician. Because of this, their cottage at the beach remained vacant. Rita had a suggestion for Rosa. "If you are interested," she started, "I can give you a deal on a summer rental for most of the season. Shane's condition requires that we stay here until the end of August, and we don't have the energy to prepare and market the place. You would have to open and clean the house and bring bedding and towels. Are you interested?"

The offer opened up the possibility of an unforgettable summer at the beach. The prospect was enticing. "I'll take it," she said immediately. "I believe my roommates will be interested, and if we split it four ways, it will be very affordable."

" I will give you the keys and tell the neighbors you will be there."

Rita's neighbors were retired and watched the Murphy's bungalow. They were always home, which was a blessing, but they could be intrusive and sometimes complained about the vacation rentals. They were sensitive to noise at night, so any loud partying would have to occur before 10 pm. That was not an issue for Rosa, who was often in bed by 10 pm. Rosa stayed at the lake that night, excited about the summer and the cute little cottage that would be her vacation space.

***

When Tammy realized Alex was spending his Saturday night at home, she asked him to take Lawrence so she could have a grown-up dinner with Carl. Alex tried to hide his smile as he answered her. "Of course. Can I take him to the bowling alley and the pizza place?"

"Sure. I appreciate it, Al."

"No problem. I'm sure you and Carl have some catching up to do."

"I know Lawrence will be eager to bowl with you."

Lawrence was chatty that night, and armed with questions for Alex. "Is that lady your girlfriend yet?"

"I'm working on it, Lawrence. I took her to the beach last Saturday."

"Is she a good swimmer?"

"She can swim like a fish."

"Lucky!" Lawrence smiled. "I think Carl wants to be Mommy's boyfriend."

"Really?"

"He took us to dinner, and I saw him holding her hand."

Alex didn't think this was any of his business, so he tried to change the subject. "Where did you go for dinner?"

"Falls View. Carl ordered a hot dog 'all the way', but I had mine plain."

Falls View was a popular hamburger and hot dog place across the street from the Passaic Falls. 'All the way' had so many toppings you could barely find the hot dog. Alex imagined the description was the owner's little joke. Lawrence enjoyed his pizza and said it was almost as good as Falls View. Bowling was an adventure; Lawrence played with side bumpers, and Alex used them too since he was a terrible bowler. After two games, they called it a night. When Lawrence asked if he could sleep over, Alex called Tammy from the bowling alley so he would not interrupt their grown-up dinner. When Alex drove Lawrence back to the house, Tammy had left Lawrence's pajamas and toothbrush in the hallway. He slept on the couch in Buster and Cleo's room. Lawrence put a new toy in their cage and was delighted to see them frolicking in the water.

"Do you think they're on a date?" he asked.

"Maybe." Alex distracted him with a game of cards, since he thought that Tammy should answer questions about male-female interactions. The 9:30 bedtime saved Alex from further discussion. He tucked Lawrence in, retired to his room, and was quiet so Lawrence would go to sleep. He pulled a romance novel from his nightstand, and after reading for an hour, dozed off earlier than usual. Alex heard the bed upstairs around midnight. He couldn't believe Carl would move so fast, or that Tammy would be willing. Alex felt like a peeping Tom lying in his bed. On any other night he would move to the couch, but Lawrence was sleeping there. He heard them several times that night and realized after years of longing they must be desperate for each other. He thought about Rosa and wished he could call her. She had been on his mind every night since that passionate encounter in December; she was the only woman who slept in his bedroom; the only woman he wanted to be with. He suffered at the thought that she could be with him right now. Tammy and Carl were upstairs enjoying each other, but it would mortify Tammy if she knew Alex could hear them. In the morning, Alex distracted Lawrence with the care of the birds since he didn't know if Tammy and Carl planned to sleep in. Carl knocked on the door, bringing donuts.

"How was your sleepover, Lawrence?" he asked as he helped himself to coffee.

"Great," replied Lawrence. "Alex and I had so much fun. How was yours?"

Tammy was standing in the doorway, flustered, but Carl answered honestly. "We had fun too."

The love affair between Tammy and Carl was official. Alex suspected it was more than a fling. Carl was a nice guy, dependable, and good with Lawrence. The attraction was surprising, but they had thought about each other for many years. Alex took a nap after they left, then showered since he had a date with Rosa for her birthday.

***

Alex arrived at the house and said hello to Connie, Chrissy, and Charlie. The topic of discussion was the cottage at the shore; Alex thought it sounded fun and hoped Rosa would ask him to visit. Rosa dressed in straight-leg jeans, a white button-down blouse, and white Keds. She was stunning in the simple outfit. Rosa's beauty was natural, and Alex had trouble keeping his eyes off of her while driving. When they arrived at the dance school, she was confused.

"Is this the surprise activity, Alex?"

"Your present is here. Why don't you come in?"

He guided her to the smaller studio, and a present sat in the middle of the room, wrapped in heart paper with a single red rose on top of the package.

"Is that for me?"

"Happy birthday, Rosa."

She was thrilled when she opened the present. The tap shoes were top quality, a brand used by professional dancers. She knew how expensive they were. "Alex, I'm not worthy."

He smiled. "Try them on."

They were comfortable, and the sound was amazing.

"Show me what you've got, Rosa."

"Alex, it's been years."

"A simple time step will do."

She was tentative but able to achieve a clear, crisp sound. Alex was putting on his tap shoes. "Show me what you've got, Alex."

His moves and sound were reminiscent of the dance movies she loved. He performed like Donald O'Connor or Ray Bolger; a clean, crisp sound and a sense of fun and comedy when he danced. He was amazing.

"Alex, I can't believe you're not famous."

"I know a company of tap dancers who love what they do but will never be rich and famous. They are the purists of rhythm tap, and it's all about the sound. They occasionally get parts in movies and shows but rarely get fairly compensated for their dedication and talent. I recently joined this tap company; I'm the only white guy in the group."

"Are there women in the group?"

"Only two. Anyway, I hope you join my summer tap class and consider occasionally joining me in a duo."

"Alex, I could never tap like that."

"You could gain confidence and learn choreography from me. We look perfect together, Rosa, like Fred Astaire and Ginger Rogers. We already have ballroom experience; adding tap is something we could do. Fred and Ginger were the most famous dance couple. Fred was the dancer, and Ginger was an actress who could dance; she was exceptional because she made dancing with him look like the most thrilling experience imaginable."

She gave him a steamy kiss. "Dancing with you, Alex, is the most thrilling experience imaginable. No acting required."

He wondered if she was talking about dancing, but kept his desires in check and focused on tap. After an hour, she showed improvement. They had an early dinner, and Alex brought her home afterward. He gave her a gentle goodnight kiss. "Happy birthday, Rosa. The tap class is on Wednesday night at 7. It is a small group; two other women with a tap background and a teenage boy who has shown amazing progress in the last year. I expect it to be a lot of fun."

"Thanks, Alex, I'll be there. This birthday has been amazing."

Chapter 27

The ocean-themed cottage was on the bay. It had two bedrooms, a kitchen, a living room, a bathroom, and a large screened porch. A breeze from the bay cooled the rooms, especially at night. The screened porch was on the bay side and was perfect for a party, and an outdoor shower and patio with a grill were off the side of the porch. Rosa and Chrissy arrived on Thursday night to air out the place. After opening the windows, the stuffiness of being closed up during the winter months diminished. They played rock tunes while making the beds with fresh linens and light quilts, cleaned the bathroom, stocked fresh towels, and rinsed the kitchenware. By 10 pm, they had the place set up the way they wanted. They went to bed early, slept soundly, and rose with the sun. After stopping at a local coffee shop for breakfast, they went food shopping. Rosa and Chrissy worked well together; the place was clean, comfortable, and stocked with groceries. After lunch, they headed for the beach. Both women were stunning in bathing suits, but Rosa was not there to sunbathe. She coaxed Chrissy into the cold water, but Chrissy couldn't stay in and gave Rosa an apologetic look.

"You should have asked Alex down this weekend. He's the only one who can keep up with you."

"I thought it would be nice to have a weekend for us, Chrissy."

"I know what you're thinking, Rosa. I would be the only one without a date this weekend. Don't worry about me; I'm sure I could find someone to hang out with me on the beach tomorrow. Why don't you call Alex?"

"It's too late to call now."

"It's not too late, Rosa. Tell him to bring Russ. I'm sure I could keep him entertained."

"I'm sure you could too. But honestly, I don't think Russ is looking for a summer fling. He's turning thirty, is looking for a house, and acts like he's ready to settle down. He's not like the guys you have been dating. Alex told me Russ has a thing for you, Chrissy, and I don't want him to misunderstand. Maybe asking him to come down would be misleading."

"Let him know I'm not interested in dating right now. I won't lead him on, and I won't date him unless I'm ready to take him seriously."

When Rosa called Alex, he was eager to spend another day at the beach with Rosa. He told her he thought Russ could come too. Russ worked late that night.

"Russ, I've been trying to reach you."

"I had an emergency call, Al. I worked for ten hours today. What's up?"

"How about a trip to the shore tomorrow?"

"I don't know; I had a rough week."

"I'll drive so you can sleep in the car. I'm meeting Rosa, and Chrissy needs a companion."

"In that case, I'm in. Make up the couch for me. I'm staying over."

"Do you want a chocolate under the pillow too?"

"That would be nice. By the way, was this your idea?"

"No, it was Chrissy's, but don't get excited. She's not interested in dating right now."

"Oh, and you all figured I was a safe choice."

"Something like that. Cheer up, Russ. You can look at her in a bathing suit all day tomorrow."

"That could be wonderful, or it could be torture."

"I know what you mean, Russ."

***

The guys started early and planned to meet the girls near the Third Street lifeguard stand. They were late because of the traffic. They unpacked their gear and headed for the beach, and as soon as Rosa saw them, she stood up and pointed to the ocean. Russ whispered to Alex on the way over.

"Rosa was a pretty girl, but now, wow, she sure can fill out a bathing suit."

Alex felt annoyed with Russ for noticing Rosa's sexy look, but Alex was certain every man nearby had watched her sprinting toward the water. "Sorry, she's taken Russ. Yours is waiting for you on the blanket."

Russ looked to Chrissy, who was stunning in her black bikini. "Are you sure she's not looking to date Al?"

"That's what she said. Excuse me, I'm ready to take the plunge."

Alex threw off his shirt and ran into the water after Rosa. Russ joined Chrissy on the blanket.

"Those two are something else," he said. "I'm sure it's crazy cold out there."

"It is," replied Chrissy. "I put my feet in, and they felt numb."

"If you want to swim, I will go with you. But it will be a short dip to cool off." He sat on the blanket with her, trying not to gawk. She was that beautiful.

"So Russ, I know you're related to Alex, but I don't know anything about you. What do you do?"

Russ sighed. This is not the conversation he wished to have. "I'm a plumber."

"Really? I never went out with a plumber."

"Not too many women have."

Chrissy laughed. "You're so tall; can you manage small spaces?"

"I can. Sometimes, height can be an advantage."

"I find tall men attractive," she said, "and I guess being a plumber is cool."

Russ was already smitten. She did not seem put off by his job. He was content sitting on the blanket with her and asked about her career.

"I work on and off, Russ. I get modeling jobs when I can, but they usually want me for my hands. My steady income is as an after-school nanny, but it isn't enough to pay my bills. I like the kids, a boy and a girl; they are good kids, though spoiled. Their parents are doctors and are always working. Someday when I have kids, I would like to stay home with them."

"I didn't know there were hand models, Chrissy. Will you continue your career for several more years?"

"Probably not. I'm getting discouraged, and I just turned twenty-three. They usually look for younger models."

"Well, I would hire you right now. At twenty-three, you look perfect."

Chrissy smiled at him; he was adorable, handsome, and so transparent. She was certain he would not make any unwanted advances. Russ was different from the self-absorbed actors or the wealthy foreigners she had been meeting in New York. She appreciated this nice, intriguing older guy.

The two couples enjoyed a fun afternoon; the ridiculous stories Alex and Russ told about growing up together entertained the girls. The sandwiches were delicious, but it was a challenge to eat them on the beach because of the sand. As Alex and Rosa headed into the water, Chrissy and Russ brought beach chairs to the water's edge and enjoyed the surf. The ocean had a calming effect on Russ. He was nervous around Chrissy, but the soothing surf and Chrissy's openness gave him the courage to be himself. They savored the surf and the sky, and were astonished when they saw dolphins in the distance. A flutter interrupted their reverie, and a squawking sound closed in on them.

"Hey Chrissy, look at that gull. He has an entire bag of potato chips, and the others are trying to steal it."

"I don't blame them; that brand is my favorite."

Then, an elderly man approached them. "Excuse me, I have a beach towel next to yours, and I think that seagull just stole your potato chips."

Chrissy was astonished. "But I had them tucked away in my beach bag."

"Was the bag zipped?"

Russ and Chrissy returned to their beach blanket; the potato chips gone, their belonging scattered.

"I'm glad we already ate the sandwiches," noted Russ.

"I thought I was street smart, but I'm not beach smart."

"Where are you from, Chrissy?"

"Idaho."

"Then I guess that explains why you're disappointed about the potato chips."

She gave his arm a playful squeeze. At that moment, their friendship began.

Rosa and Alex finally dried off, salty and exhausted. When they returned to the beach house, Charlie was already starting the charcoal grill. They gathered for dinner, and as the guys talked sports, the girls listened to Mary Lou go on and on about her recent engagement to Lewis. The roommates were happy for her, but relieved when she left the party early. There was only so much wedding talk one could take. Around 10 pm, Rosa suggested Alex and Russ spend the night on the porch. Rosa was concerned about the long drive back and the beer drinking. Rosa, always prepared, had brought extra toothbrushes and floss. As they conversed as couples, they whispered and sat close, but because of the soft jazz music, the active day, and the lack of privacy, they all dozed off by midnight.

***

Rosa awakened early in the morning, and Connie was already making coffee. Rosa was in Alex's arms; he was sleeping, but his hand was on her breast. He was such a guy. Russ and Chrissy were asleep and looked adorable together. Everything seemed right on this sunny Sunday in June. The smell of coffee and the freshness of the sea breeze invigorated her as she looked forward to another epic day. They were all so content. Rosa prayed summer would always be like this, but realized this brief moment of perfection might not last.

Chapter 28

After a wonderful weekend, the group left the cottage, but Chrissy stayed behind. The family she worked for was on vacation, so she had two weeks off from her nanny job. She appreciated her vacation pay; since she was part time, they were not obligated to give it, but finances were tight and she was grateful for the unexpected paycheck. Her employers wanted to reward her for the extra hours she stayed when asked and appreciated how well she cared for their children. The two weeks at the shore gave her time to relax and reevaluate her goals. After high school graduation, Chrissy's father wanted to send her to college for a degree, but she insisted she try modeling and acting in New York. She had limited success with modeling jobs, but not enough to jump-start a career, and now she was being passed over for younger girls. Women with a more exotic look were being considered for most jobs. Her all-American, blond-haired, blue-eyed girl-next-door look was not as popular as it had been a few years earlier. She spent the week alone, reading novels and driving to the beach every morning. Interested men approached her, and though she was polite, it was obvious she was not available. She was there to relax and get a tan, and after a few days, she was untroubled, sun-kissed, and even more attractive.

A plumbing problem that prevented her from using the bathroom in the house interrupted her vacation. She tried to fix it herself, but only made matters worse. She had to rely on the neighbor's bathroom, which was embarrassing. In desperation, she called Russ, and he cut his work week short to arrive on Friday afternoon. Chrissy met him at the door; she had emerged from the outdoor shower dressed in her terrycloth robe. Russ tried to focus on the plumbing problem, though it was hard for him to stop thinking about what Chrissy had on under the robe. She stood in the bathroom with him; he was careful to avoid looking at her and instead focused on the plumbing.

Rosa also arrived at the cottage that afternoon, surprised to see an unfamiliar vehicle in the driveway. It was a work van; a little beat up with no markings on the outside. She was concerned that Chrissy hadn't called to tell her that workers were on the premises. As she entered through the front door, the place looked empty, but she heard running water in the bathroom.

"Hello?" No answer. Then she heard a man's voice, and it sounded like Russ.

"I think you need to move over, Chrissy."

"There's not enough room in here," she complained. "The stupid door opens the wrong way."

"I thought you were going to help," he grumbled.

"Do we have to do this right now?" she asked.

"Well, you're the one who asked me to come in," he said defensively.

"Honestly, Russ, I thought you would be good at this. Maybe you should start over."

He paused. "No, this isn't going to work." Then Russ whispered, sounding exasperated. "I'm sorry you're dissatisfied with my performance. Maybe you should get dressed and let me finish this myself."

Rosa was embarrassed to be eavesdropping and had her hand on the door. She tried to leave. She couldn't believe what she was hearing. Then Chrissy emerged in her robe.

"Oh, hi Rosa. I didn't know you were here. Do you need to get into the bathroom?"

Rosa blushed. She was ready to burst after the two-hour car ride. "No thanks, Chrissy. I can wait."

"Are you sure? You look uncomfortable."

Just then, Russ emerged wearing his tool belt and had a shower curtain rod in hand. "Hi, Rosa. You can use the toilet, but we will have to use the outdoor shower until we can get a replacement rod for the bathroom. I want to take you girls to the diner, then to Rickles. I can get the hardware I need, and you two can shop for a new shower curtain. This one has seen better days."

"Sure Russ. Can I use the bathroom now?"

"Just watch your step; the floor is wet."

Rosa needed time to compose herself. The image created when she overheard the plumbing conversation embarrassed her. It wasn't hard to envision Chrissy and Russ together. She was relieved to see Russ dressed with his tool belt on. The girls dressed for a casual dinner; Chrissy was ready first since she had already showered. The three of them had fun at the diner, and their domestic shopping trip was a novel way to spend a Friday night. Russ was right at home at Rickles since it stocked items used by contractors. It had a small section for home decor, and though most of the place was full of nuts and bolts, the selection of curtains, rugs, and lamps was interesting enough to keep the girls occupied. When they returned to the cottage, it was early, so they played cards.

When Alex arrived that night, they were drinking beer at the card table. "Strip poker?" he asked hopefully.

"Sorry, Al," said Russ. "I think these two will need more beer before convincing them to do that."

Alex joined them, and they partied on the porch until midnight. Chrissy announced she was going in to get a good night's sleep, and Rosa followed her. Alex and Russ sat in silence for a few minutes until they were sure both girls were in for the night. They ventured onto the patio.

"Would you like another beer, Al?"

"A shot would be better."

"We have vodka."

"That's fine. I'll take the beer too."

They sat and enjoyed the cool bay breeze. The moon was full. "I can't believe this. Two gorgeous blonds are inside, and I'm sitting here with you."

"You are not my first choice either, Al."

"I assumed they would at least stay on the porch with us."

"Last time we had a full house. Since there are four of us, the situation is ... risky."

They downed the shot and chased it with a bottle of Bud. Russ gave Alex a thoughtful look. "Do you think men and women can be friends?"

The question surprised him. "I suppose it's possible, but most of the time no unless they are both romantically attached to someone else. Usually, one of the parties is suppressing an attraction to the other." He sighed. "Is this about you and Chrissy?"

"I doubt I will ever date someone as exciting as Chrissy."

"Don't you feel you're dating now?"

"No, she treats me like a big brother."

"Are you sure, Russ? I noticed the way she looks at you; I'd say she would consider dating."

"It's no use; she's not what I'm looking for. She's too young, and I'm ready to settle down. I imagined I would find a woman who is interested in the same things."

"If she wants to, why not have a summer romance? It doesn't have to be serious, and it's not like you would be her first boyfriend. You can enjoy it as long as you both want the relationship."

"There's a problem, Al. Of course, she's amazing, and I can't believe she wants to spend time with me. But it is becoming more than physical attraction; I like her and am getting used to being with her. She's sweet, sassy, and somehow vulnerable too. I think she's been with guys who want to show her off without getting to know her. I feel comfortable with her, and like her even when we argue about stupid things like the rod for the shower curtain. When she bosses me around, I act insulted but honestly think it's funny; she takes a genuine interest in what I am doing."

"And that works for you?"

"It does."

"You don't know Russ, maybe her wants are the same as yours. Forget about age; relax and see what happens."

Alex finished his beer. Russ's exposed feelings surprised him, and Alex decided to open up too. "This friendship first is killing me. Rosa has shaken my self-confidence."

Russ looked at him with sympathy. "Take the advice you gave me, Al, and be patient, relax, to see what happens. Women are built differently; they don't seem to care as much about sex."

"It depends on the girl."

"Do you think so?"

"When I slept with Rosa, which, by the way, is on my mind every single day, it was her idea and her call. She pursued me and was more anxious than I was. It was a turn-on that she wanted me so much. She enjoyed the night as much as I did, maybe even more."

"Then I think it will happen, Al. In the meantime, the two of us will learn to survive on the tiny morsels they are willing to give us."

"I hope we don't starve, Russ. I'm getting hungry."

Chapter 29

The dental clinic at the geriatric hospital was closed for a two-week vacation. Dottie spent time with her daughter's family and seemed like she needed a vacation from her vacation. Her three grandchildren were young and active, and Dottie's daughter depended on her to babysit. She loved them, but was happy to resume her normal work schedule. Rosa worked extra hours to accommodate emergencies that had waited for her return, and after a hectic day, Rosa stopped by Dr. Ryan's office to say hello. He was at his desk, lost in his thoughts. He looked terrible. Rosa was concerned and closed the door behind her.

"Is something wrong, Gerry?" she asked with a panicked voice. "You're not sick, are you?"

"No, Rosa, not physically, but emotionally I'm drained. Working at the AIDS clinic has taken a toll. I lost another friend this week."

"I'm so sorry, Gerry."

He had deep sadness in his eyes. Then he glanced at her. "You, my dear, look fantastic. The beach agrees with you."

"You should visit and take your mind off your work. It's amazing how peaceful the ocean can be."

"Thanks, but I'm not a beach person."

Rosa assumed everyone liked the beach. "Well, maybe we can do something else."

"I'm afraid I'm not good company right now. I plan to attend a memorial service later this week, which will be difficult. But I miss talking to you. How about going for coffee next week?"

"Of course, Gerry, whatever works for you." She looked at this colleague she had grown close to. She wanted to help. "Take care of yourself, Gerry. I know you feel obligated to work with AIDS patients, but maybe it is leading to depression."

"I suspect it is. Hopefully, I am through the worst of it; I lost two close friends. I was desperate to save them, but now they're gone, and it's time to focus on myself. I have not taken risks and continue to test negative."

"Many people depend on you, Gerry. The best thing you could do for everyone is take care of yourself."

"I will, Rosa. I look forward to our coffee date next week. Hopefully, I will get sleep and be myself again."

***

Rosa was eager to attend the first tap class. She joined three other students; Dee, a waitress in her forties who had danced most of her life, Madison, a college girl studying to be a nurse, and Pedro, a high school junior into break dancing, a motley crew with different levels of talent. Alex brought them together and incorporated the goals and interests of each student. Rosa and Dee trained traditionally, while Madison and Pedro were more cutting-edge and contemporary. They enjoyed Alex's choreography because the sound was amazing; tapping was music and the instrument was the tap shoe. He used big band songs, hip-hop, jazz, and rock; forever challenging, pushing their limits, and bringing them out of their comfort zone. The class was a blast; creative and rewarding.

The following week, the class was even better. They focused on Michael Jackson's music, and Alex and Pedro showed their moon-walking skills. Alex choreographed a dance using a Michael Jackson song, and the students agreed his choice was perfect for the group. They were in a lively discussion when Jackie interrupted the class. Rosa had a phone call. It was Connie. Rosa was concerned; Connie usually waited until Rosa was home to talk to her.

"Hi, Rosa. Your mother called looking for you. Your father had a heart attack, and the ambulance brought him to St. Joseph's Hospital. He is in intensive care but stable; your mother thought you might want to go to the hospital to see him."

When Rosa returned to class, she looked pale. "Alex, I have to go. My father is in the hospital."

"I'll take you," he insisted. "You're too upset to drive."

"Go ahead, Alex," offered Jackie. "I will close the studio tonight."

They didn't talk on the way to the hospital. Rosa was grateful for the ride. They found the ICU and met Anita in the waiting area.

"How is he, Mom?"

"He is stable, but the doctor said he will stay in the hospital for several days. Would you like to go in? They allow a few minutes."

"Sure, Mom. Thanks for the ride, Alex; I don't expect you to stay since I don't know how long I will be here."

"Go ahead, Rosa. We'll talk about it after you see him."

Alex and Anita sat together in the waiting room. She knew how much Oliver depended on Alex, and her opinion of him had softened.

She thought Alex might tell her what was wrong at the office, since she knew her husband had been under stress.

"Alex, I have never seen him so stressed about work. He won't talk about it, and I know it's not the usual tax season stress; it's not tax season anymore."

"I probably shouldn't say anything, but you will find out anyway, and have the right to know since it involves your family. Mr. Diaz made a few errors while filing one of the corporate accounts, and the IRS has scheduled an audit. The client is understandably upset, and our office is under investigation. Although the mistakes were honest, there might be legal problems for the firm."

Anita was furious. "My father should have retired years ago, I told Oliver I had noticed a problem with his memory. But nobody listens to me. I wanted Oliver to sell the business so we could move beyond the sacrifices of being self-employed."

"I'm sure he doesn't want to sell. He has talked about bringing in a partner, but I am not a candidate since I am not a CPA and don't want to pursue that career path. I may be able to handle the audit for him. If we are lucky, the penalty will be a small fine since there was no criminal intent."

"I hope you're right." As Anita looked at him, she was both grateful and apologetic. "I'm sorry I called you a fairy, Alex."

He smiled. "I'm not that sensitive, Mrs. Fletcher. Besides, you were only being truthful." He winked, and Anita realized it was impossible to dislike him. She could see why her daughter was smitten with his charm.

Rosa appeared relieved when she returned to the waiting room. "He's in good spirits but worried about the business. He wants to talk to Alex tomorrow morning. I think I will stay here, Alex. Mom can drive me to the dance studio to get my car."

"Are you sure? I don't mind staying or driving you."

"No, get some sleep. He will need you in the morning, and will have anxiety until he puts his business affairs in order."

"Please call if you need anything. I don't care what time it is."

"Thanks, Alex."

***

Alex was hesitant to leave Rosa at the hospital. After he drove home, he settled on the couch in the living room so he could hear the phone. The parakeets were cranky. They were used to lights out and blankets on by 10 pm. He read for a while before falling asleep. The phone rang at 1 am. Rosa was calling from a payphone.

"Rosa, how's your dad?"

"He's fine, but I'm not. Can you pick me up at the hospital?"

"I'm on my way."

He wondered why Rosa needed the ride but didn't ask questions. He saw her at the entrance before he had a chance to park. Rosa's smudged eye makeup suggested she had been crying. He drove to the entrance. "Rosa, what's wrong?"

"I'll tell you later." She was on the verge of tears and unable to explain. "Just take me home."

They drove in silence as he made his way onto Route 80. "You're going the wrong way, Alex."

"You're just tired, Rosa. I'm going the right way."

"You misunderstood. I want to go to your home. It's much closer to the hospital."

He made a U-turn and proceeded to his place, not asking questions. He led her in, and they walked to the living room. "Can I make you a warm drink? It might make you feel better: warm milk or hot apple tea?"

"What is hot apple tea?"

"Just something Nana used to give us kids. She would pour apple juice into a teacup and add hot water. It's warm and sweet and comforting."

"Apple tea sounds delicious."

He sat waiting patiently for an explanation. Finally, she opened up to him. "I made an earth-shattering discovery at the hospital. Oliver Fletcher is not my biological father."

"Are you sure, Rosa? Maybe there's been a mistake."

"There is no mistake. I read his chart and noticed his blood type. I approached the night nurse and asked if it was an error. A previous visit confirmed the blood type. There is no way he can be my biological father."

"There could be confusion about your blood type."

"In undergraduate, we tested blood type in genetics lab. I was also told my blood type when I had my tonsils out."

"Did you ask your mother?"

"I did. She gave me a bullshit answer and told me I didn't know what I was talking about." Rosa was so upset she had trouble speaking. "I always knew something was wrong. I'm so much taller than everyone else in the family; why am I the only tall one? I'm twenty-seven years old. Why didn't she tell me?" She burst into tears.

Alex held her and encouraged her to sip the apple tea. He knew the heartache of never meeting his father or his mother. Finally, the tears stopped. He stroked her hair as she clung to him. "Why don't you get some rest? I have comfy pajamas you can wear and a new toothbrush; the one you gave me at my last appointment."

"Never mind, Alex. I have one in my purse. I'm sure you need the toothbrush, since it has been months since your dental visit."

She washed her face and dressed in men's pajamas. When she was ready, he tucked her in like a little girl and kissed her forehead. "Try to get a good night's sleep. We'll drive to the hospital in the morning."

His mind was racing as he stretched out on the couch. He wondered why families had to be so screwed up. Even Russ's model family, with two parents who stayed together, seemed perfect but had their own problems. He tossed and turned and decided a warm shower might help him get to sleep. He was quiet so that he wouldn't disturb Rosa. Then, he heard a soft knock on the door.

"Alex, can I come in?"

"Come in."

He wondered if she needed something in the bathroom. She pulled back the shower curtain and stepped in with him. She stood naked before him, and he embraced her while moving her into the warm stream of cascading water. His body responded immediately, but he hesitated, unsure of how he should act. The night had been exhausting and emotional, and this was unexpected. He kissed her so sweetly, gently. He smoothed body wash over her silky skin, savoring her beauty and softness. Alex wanted to wash away her tears and take care of her. Finally, he turned the shower off and wrapped her in a fluffy white towel. She took his hand and led him into the hallway. She stopped. He followed her lead. She wanted to be lifted, and they started to make love. She needed an escape, and he was there to give her what she needed.

His composure in the shower surprised her. She lost her control when they entered the hallway, and she took him passionately even though he warned her he was not going to last. As she seduced him, she felt connected to him and couldn't control her overwhelming desire to give him pleasure. He had always enjoyed sex, but this was electric. She moved like a dancer and was incredibly soft; she didn't hold back, and Alex was sure a woman had never wanted him as much as she did. He enjoyed her movements and finally yielded to their sizzling intercourse. He maintained his hold on her, though he felt he had lost his strength. "I'm sorry, Rosa, I couldn't control myself."

She smiled, ran her fingers through his hair, and kissed him passionately. "It's all right, Alex. I know how much you like me."

The truth is, he loved her, but thought it was too soon to tell her.

"You're not tired, are you?" she asked.

"No, I'm never too tired to be with you."

She picked up the towel and hurried toward the bedroom. When he reached the doorway, she was seductively sprawled across the bed, her body embraced by the moonlight and flushed by their rendezvous in the hallway. He savored the vision and tried to commit it to memory; he was captured by her sex appeal and in awe of her feminine beauty. When he slipped into bed beside her, he touched and caressed her and was soon ready to immerse himself in her softness. She felt a need for him and immediately responded. After her initial waves of pleasure, he continued to indulge her, transporting her to a place beyond thought, space, and time. He wasn't sure where she went, but wanted to go with her. His explosive release completed them, and the intensity of their passion gripped Alex. When she thanked him repeatedly, he knew the experience was also extraordinary for her. He fell asleep, but with a tight hold on her as he nestled behind her. Rosa suspected he feared she might leave. This time she was not going anywhere. The magnetism was remarkable, and when coupled with their friendship and emotional bond, Rosa felt like she had found her silver lining in a world full of heartache. Alex had become everything; her lover, escape, and friend, and she felt complete when she was in his arms. When they awakened, it was early enough to enjoy morning sex that was sleepy and satisfying. She still needed his closeness and his warmth. They reluctantly left his bedroom to face the challenges of the day.

***

When they entered the bright, sunny kitchen, Buster and Cleopatra's happy sounds greeted them as soon as Alex removed the blanket from their cage. Alex brewed coffee; the caffeine energized them and was much needed after only a few hours of sleep. Rosa sat at the table while Alex served fruit, cereal, and hard-boiled eggs. They looked up when they heard a flutter in the cage; it was obvious what was happening. Alex was surprised by this new behavior, as he had not put in a nesting box. Rosa gave him a questioning look.

"Do you think they saw us in the hallway?"

He waggled his eyebrows, then noted, "There was a blanket on the cage."

"Do you think they heard us?"

"Now that is a possibility. The door was open while we were in the shower. Carl, the parakeet expert, said the birds are from Australia and mate during the rainy season. He suggested I close the windows when it is raining."

"It was surprisingly graphic."

"I hope you enjoyed the show. I never expected to see porn this morning."

Rosa smiled at his ridiculous comment. But then she became thoughtful. "Do you think there will be eggs?"

Alex knew to tread carefully; he suspected the question was not specifically for Buster and Cleo. "I do not expect eggs yet; Cleo is young, and it's not good for the hen to produce too early. If they exhibit nesting behavior, I will give them a nesting box. Then there might be eggs; I would do everything I could to care for them. Buster and Cleo have beautiful plumage, and their offspring will have unusual markings."

Rosa looked at her hard-boiled egg. "I don't think I can eat this, Alex."

" I'll save mine too. I can make egg salad later."

Chapter 30

Dottie canceled the day at the clinic after Rosa called about her father. Alex turned on the radio as they drove to the hospital. He assumed Rosa needed time to think, and he didn't want to distract or influence her with his thoughts and concerns. She was in an awkward predicament, not knowing if Oliver was aware of her mother's indiscretion. They arrived at the start of visiting hours while the cardiologist was making rounds; the doctor suggested they keep their visit short and asked that they avoid confrontation. Alex wondered whether a discussion about the audit with Mr. Fletcher was inappropriate. Oliver was happy to see Rosa and Alex and was determined to avoid getting upset, even though he assumed they had spent the night together. He had to relax and trust Alex with his business and his daughter. He needed to speak to Alex about the office and sent Rosa on an errand so they could talk in private.

"How are you feeling, boss?"

"Not bad. This happens when you dwell on problems that are beyond your control. I allowed the audit to consume me."

"Maybe something predisposed you to the heart attack. It's fortunate you recognized it as serious."

"I want to talk about work," said Oliver.

"Are you sure? The doctor advised against it."

"I will be more upset if I lie here wondering what will happen next. Can you reschedule the audit?"

"I can try if that's what you want, but you should let me handle the audit. Your health is more important."

"You might not be able to provide them with all the information they need, and the IRS could take away my CPA license."

"I'm sure they will understand you are in the hospital and cannot keep the appointment. If I meet them, I can present records that have nothing to do with me since the errors happened before I joined the company. As an uninvolved party, I wouldn't misrepresent the client's assets or hide mistakes. I also don't have a CPA license to consider. Sometimes it's best to have a representative meet with the auditor. That way you can hire a lawyer later if you have to, and your statements are not on the record."

"You are right, Alex. If we are lucky, Ms. Smith will conduct the audit. She set up the appointment on the phone and seemed fair and pleasant. I imagine her to be a nice, middle-aged lady. She will like you; I have seen you have a way with women, Alex."

"A woman raised me, and I spent my youth in a dance studio. Of course I'm comfortable with them."

Oliver gave him a sad smile. "I intend to talk to Rosa about a personal matter. Will you be here?"

"I will take care of her, Mr. Fletcher. You know how I feel about her."

At that moment, Rosa entered the room with the herbal tea Oliver had ordered. Alex gave her a cautious glance and tried to warn her of the private conversation that was to follow.

"Take your time, Rosa. I'll be in the waiting room."

Olive had a big smile for her. "How's my favorite girl?"

She tried to compose herself. "I'm so worried about you, Daddy."

"Rosa, we have to talk."

"I don't want to discuss anything that will upset you."

"We need to talk now in case my condition gets worse. My heart attack has been a reminder of how unpredictable life can be, and I'm afraid if something happens to me, you will never know the truth. You have the right to know what happened before you were born. This talk is overdue."

Rosa could hardly breathe. She already knew what this was about.

"It's a long story, and I can only provide the details I have. Your mother will have to fill in the blanks."

"I'm ready, Dad." She waited patiently as he sipped his tea.

"My father and Mr. Diaz graduated from college together and started the accounting firm. I visited the office as a child, and by high school, I decided I also wanted to pursue a career in accounting. I worked at the firm after college, and the business grew. I was thirty years old when the partners approached me with a proposition. Mr. Diaz's daughter, your mother, was in trouble. She had graduated from high school and was working as a secretary. She was pregnant. I don't know anything about your biological father, except that he died in a car accident during his freshman year of college. They asked if I would consider a marriage arrangement so that your mother and the baby would have a home. I agreed. I was an awkward young man and had no experience dating women. I assumed I would remain a bachelor and couldn't believe this Cuban beauty was willing to be my wife. We were married in the Catholic Church and barely knew each other. It wasn't easy. Anita was too young to be married, and I didn't know what to do with her. She was distraught and unhappy. But then you were born, and from that moment on I knew I loved you with all my heart. I was destined to be your father, and I prayed for the poor soul who fathered you and would never have the chance to meet you. It didn't matter that I was not there at conception. You were, and are, in every way my child. If it were up to me, I would have told you as soon as you were old enough to understand. Your mother didn't see the point in telling you since your birth father was gone, and it was not my place to insist."

"Oh Dad, I thank God it was you. Don't worry about me. I'm glad to know the truth."

"Please don't judge your mother too harshly. She was young and frightened, but made an adult decision to make a home for you. As a couple, we were not compatible, but as parents, we thrived. It is because of you that we stayed together. We hoped that having more children would bring us closer, but God had other plans, and after a while, we knew there would be just the three of us. We are so proud and grateful to have you."

"I love you so much, Daddy."

"I love you too, Rosa. Please make peace with your mother; right now she's afraid to talk to you. After staying here all night, she finally went home to get some sleep."

"I promise I will try."

Rosa visited her dad the next day after work, and he looked well-rested and his condition had improved. The doctors expected he would be home by the weekend. Rosa said hello to her mother, but they did not talk. Rosa's focus was her father's recovery, and because she didn't want to upset him, she kept all questions to herself.

***

The weather forecast was for rain and storms as the last weekend of the cottage rental approached. The other roommates were done with the rental; Charlie kept Connie busy with his weekend events; Chrissy and Mary Lou were not speaking to each other and would not vacation in the same space. Rosa asked Alex to drive with her. Even though the rain might keep them off the beach, it would be a chance to get away and spend the weekend alone. The weather was nice enough to swim on Saturday morning. The lifeguards were at their stations, but there were few vacationers since the day was stormy. Alex and Rosa swam most of the morning; the churning surf was warm and bubbly and felt like a spa. They left when it started to rain. As they removed their wet bathing suits and lay naked on the porch, they spent quiet time in conversation and intimacy. Rosa tried to be discreet about sharing the outdoor shower, but she was sure the neighbors noticed they were there for a long time. Alex had become Rosa's best friend. He understood the loss she felt not knowing her biological father, and she did not want to discuss it with anyone else.

Magic was in the air as they lay together on the porch. At dusk, they could hear the waves lapping against the rocky shore and frogs singing in the tall grass. The air was salty, and torrential rain flooded the streets. The way Alex made her feel was overwhelming. He listened and responded to her, and she knew she would be lonely without him. She had to admit she was falling in love. They rested in each other's arms, the constant sound of the rainstorm lulling them into a deep, satisfied sleep. Buster and Cleo would have appreciated the rhythm of the night.

Chapter 31

Anita was awake at dawn on Sunday morning. She was eager to bring her husband home from the hospital, and she planned to arrive early so that he could be one of the first patients discharged. She chose a pastel print sundress from her closet and spent additional time on her hair and makeup. When she viewed her image in the mirror, she looked attractive. Anita was forty-six years old but appeared younger since she was slim and petite. Oliver's stay in the hospital seemed like an eternity to her, and she realized how lonely she was without him. His heart attack frightened her; the thought of losing him haunted her, especially at night. Oliver had always taken care of her, and for twenty-seven years she had taken him for granted. She remembered the early days of their marriage and how she had longed for her freedom. Now she didn't want it. Her parents had forced her into a situation she was sure would lead to unhappiness, but they chose an honest man who loved her and Rosa with all his heart. After many years, she realized she had nothing to complain about; she was content.

She spent the days at home preparing the family room for Oliver's return. The room was the most interesting space in the house. Double sliders led to a patio that overlooked the lake. A large rustic bar with an oak counter lined a side wall, though Oliver didn't drink. Anita loved to entertain, and the bar was a gathering place for neighbors and weekend guests. A brick fireplace was the chief attraction in the winter months, but in the summer the cool breezes, the lake view, and access to the patio made it the perfect place for Oliver's recovery. Oliver had a home office next to the family room, so when he was ready to work again, his accounts were accessible. Anita used a sheet set and a light summer quilt on the couch and added extra pillows since the doctor said he would sleep more comfortably if propped up.

Oliver had gone against her wishes and disclosed a past she wanted to keep hidden, but Anita realized they should have told Rosa a long time ago. Rosa deserved to know the truth; and it was deceptive to keep it from her. Rosa grew up thinking she was English when she did not have a drop of English blood in her background. She was Cuban and Polish, a combination that resulted in an exotic, unique look. She was pretty in an unconventional way, and it was hard to guess her heritage. Rosa assumed her calm, measured disposition was from Oliver, but perhaps her biological father also had these traits. The drama Miss Jackie had noted in childhood most definitely came from her mother. Anita had seen her daughter dancing with Alex and assumed Rosa's passionate side would surface when she was with him.

When Anita entered the hospital room, Oliver's heart skipped a beat. She had dressed up to take him home. He hoped that during the weeks of recovery he could reconnect with the woman he loved. Oliver seemed to improve with age. The only change to his hair was a hint of grey near his temples. He had a few wrinkles around his eyes from the sun while fishing on the lake. He had the look of an accountant, bookish and reserved, but dimples gave him a boyish appearance, and Anita had become attracted to him. She had also fallen in love with him, and the thought of losing him left an ache in her heart. He was older than she was, and she thought she might someday be alone, but she couldn't face it. Anita was determined to put more effort into nurturing their relationship. She hadn't been an easy wife, but Oliver rarely lost his temper and was usually patient and understanding. He appreciated her. They couldn't stop smiling as the nurse wheeled him to the hospital entrance for his release. Oliver couldn't wait to return to his home on the lake.

***

Carl and Lawrence finished dinner and went downstairs to care for the birds. Lawrence had started his bird-sitting job. It was the first time Alex had asked him to be a bird sitter, and it was the perfect chance for Lawrence to take responsibility. Alex was thankful he could leave Buster and Cleo when he spent a weekend away with Rosa. The birds were chirping and playing in the water. Then, Lawrence witnessed a new behavior and asked Carl about it. Carl hesitated, then made an excuse to go upstairs.

"Don't worry, Lawrence. It's just something that birds do. Maybe you could get two ginger ales for us. I will be back in a few minutes."

Carl hurried upstairs to talk to Tammy and asked, "What have you discussed with Lawrence about boys and girls and biology?"

"Nothing yet. Why?"

"Because he's asking for an explanation. Buster and Cleo are mating."

"Oh dear, I don't want to talk to Lawrence about those things. You can tell him whatever you think is appropriate for his age."

"And what if he asks questions about us?"

"Tell him whatever you think is appropriate."

"He needs a father."

"I know." Tammy gave him a hopeful look.

Carl had visions of doing this in a different place, at a different time, and in a different way, but before he could think he was down on one knee, unprepared but with no doubt in his mind. "Tammy, I would love to be your husband and adopt Lawrence; that is, if you want me to. Will you be my wife?"

Tammy was shocked and had tears in her eyes. This was happening so fast. "Question, Carl. Is this because of Lawrence or because of me?"

He didn't hesitate. "I have been in love with you since I was 17. Now that I know Lawrence, I love him too. I love you both with all my heart. Will you marry me?"

She started to cry. "Yes, Carl, I will marry you." She hugged him, then thought of Lawrence downstairs. "Go to Lawrence and answer his questions. I think you should stay here tonight, and we can talk later." Carl had not been staying over because they didn't want to confuse Lawrence. That changed a few moments ago.

"One more thing, Tammy. I know it's late, but can we have dessert to celebrate?"

"I have ice cream, Carl, but we'll have to deal with Lawrence and his sugar rush."

"That might be easier to deal with than questions that get too detailed. I'm not sure where this is going to go."

She smiled. Carl was already a dad. "I love you, Carl. I have chocolate ice cream; it's Lawrence's favorite."

"Mine too," he whispered after giving her a soft kiss filled with hope and promise.

Carl didn't waste any time getting a ring for Tammy. His jeweler friend had a small shop close to Carl's Bird Emporium. Tammy and Carl found the perfect ring, and when Tammy tried it on, it fit perfectly. They walked out with it that day. Tammy's friends at work were shocked, as they were not aware that Tammy was dating. They could tell by the look on her face that she was in love and sure of the life she would have with Carl. She couldn't wait to tell Alex about their plans. She hadn't seen him all week. He was gone from early morning until late at night. Alex heard a soft knock on the door as he was getting ready to go to bed. It was Tammy.

"Do you have a minute, Alex?"

"Of course, come in. Is everything all right?"

"It is. I just wanted to show you my engagement ring."

"You and Carl?"

"He asked me on Sunday night."

"Congratulations, Tammy. I'm so happy for you. The ring is beautiful."

"We never would have found each other without you and Buster. Did Carl ever mention what happened when we were in high school?"

"No, only that you went to the same high school and were in the play together."

Tammy sighed. "The story is more complicated than that, Alex."

"I'd love to hear it. How about a nightcap? "

"I'd love one. Carl is in the shower, and Lawrence is in bed. They won't miss me."

"I have beer, or wine, or sour mix. Nana used to like apricot sours. Would you like an apricot sour?"

"How exotic. Yes, please."

Alex made the drinks as Tammy started her story. "As you know, I was a freshman, and Carl, a senior. My parents were strict and told me I was not allowed to date in high school. But that didn't discourage Carl. He was always leaving notes in my locker to meet him after school. We sat outside on the bleachers and talked; sometimes he would bring me a candy bar. We found ways to spend time together, especially while practicing for the play. We were discreet since my parents would not want me to see Carl. It was all sweet and innocent, and on the night of dress rehearsal, we found ourselves alone backstage. Carl was the first boy I kissed. My fifteen-year-old heart told me I was in love. I tried to tell my mother about him, but she told me to forget it. My father would never approve because he was a senior and because of his race. She told me Dad would lock me in my room until I graduated if he ever heard about it. When my mother saw him in the play, it made things worse. Carl was a big guy with tattoos and looked like a biker. My mother was sure he intended to take advantage of an innocent young girl. I was so sad to tell Carl we couldn't see each other because of my parents. Reluctantly, he respected my wishes. I thought it was the right thing to do since everyone told me Carl was a bad choice. The funny thing is they approved of Lawrence's father, who a few years later got me pregnant and abandoned me. After that, I didn't want a relationship. I accepted my life as a single mom and occupied my time with work and with my friends in our church. I thought the chance for romance was gone from my life until I saw Carl standing in your living room. He hasn't changed. He looks tougher and stronger but still has that boyish smile that captivated me many years ago. I suspect you think this has happened fast, but our love has remained unfulfilled since high school. I know that being an interracial couple is not easy, but now that I'm older I don't care what other people think, and the social environment is beginning to change."

"That's beautiful, Tammy. I was surprised about you and Carl, but he is a good man and a good choice. I am so happy for you."

"Carl has come at the right time for Lawrence. He needs a role model, and I have always been afraid the man who fathered him would come back to bother me, perhaps asking for money or luring Lawrence into his unsavory business dealings. I know he is not far away. Carl is stable and protective; he has some tough friends who will stand by him if there is trouble. I don't think my ex would choose to mess with him."

"I don't think you have anything to worry about, Tammy. I wouldn't want to mess with Carl."

She hugged Alex so tightly it surprised him; Tammy usually showed reserve. "I love you, Alex."

"I love you too, Tammy."

Chapter 32

The weather changed late in August; hot and sticky during the day, with a temperature drop at night. Rosa always felt a sense of sadness when the summer was at its end, and though she loved the fall weather, the weeks of transition seemed depressing. The fresh green hue of spring and early summer was replaced, making everything look dry. Work was busy with back-to-school checkups and forms to fill out for school. The vacation lull had ended.

Alex was busy too, organizing his dance classes and filling in at the accounting office until Oliver could return. He spent long days at the office since Mr. Diaz worked only in the morning. Grandpa Diaz was more productive when he worked a half-day, and a strong cup of coffee helped him to focus. Ms. Smith conducted the IRS audit and determined the errors were honest mistakes. The client was required to pay back taxes with interest, and the firm had to pay a fine. As expected, Ms. Smith had a favorable impression of Alex and sympathized with Mr. Diaz, who was not as thorough as he used to be. Mr. Diaz admitted he could no longer work full-time and convinced Ms. Smith the firm would be more diligent. He promised to delegate corporate tasks in the future. Oliver was relieved that the audit was complete, and the errors resolved.

A few weeks after his return home from the hospital, Oliver was climbing stairs and taking walks around the block. He insisted on seeing his cardiologist alone since Anita dominated the conversation when she was present. When she asked about the visits, he insisted he was fine and tried to put her mind at ease. "The doctor wants me to stay at home another week," he started, "but Alex can bring accounts to me, and I will work in the home office."

Anita did not want him to overexert himself. She wished he would sell the business and retire, but Oliver knew that was not a viable option if they wanted to maintain their lifestyle. He was still too young to retire, but finding a partner made sense. Anita dreamed of travel and hoped Oliver would spend more time with her. She was concerned about his recovery. "Oliver, what did the doctor tell you?"

"He said I can work full time but be careful not to overexert myself."

"But what did he say about us?"

Oliver knew what she was talking about, but he was becoming more like Alex, and couldn't resist the urge to tease her. "What about us, Anita?"

"You know, do we have certain restrictions?"

"Do you want to know the foods I should avoid?"

"I need to know that, but that isn't what I was talking about." She felt silly and embarrassed. "Could you ask him if we can have marital relations?"

Oliver gave her a rakish grin. "I already asked Anita; it's allowed," then added, " but you have to be on top and do most of the work."

He tried to hide his dimples. The last part was a joke, but she took him seriously. Oliver left it at that.

Alex and Rosa had hectic schedules, but Alex was always ready for adventure, and Rosa was eager to join him. They canoed the Delaware River when the currents were calm and relaxing. He took Rosa on a weekend camping trip, cooked hot dogs and beans on a campfire, and slept in a tent. Alex remembered his Cub Scout days camping with his grandfather and introduced Rosa to camping. The conditions were primitive, but she thrived outdoors and even cooked a spaghetti dinner on the campfire. She was radiant in the mornings, her hair tousled, no makeup, yet looking so fresh and wholesome he couldn't resist kissing her and bringing her back into the tent. Their playground was outdoors, whether the ocean, the lakes, the woods, or moonlit nights. They were always active and happy. Their relationship was spontaneous and passionate, but Rosa suspected this gift of being together was a fleeting moment. Alex was not looking for a wife, and Rosa did not think she would marry him. They learned to embrace the present and not dwell on what would happen next.

***

The summer tap class continued into the fall semester, with the same students. Only Alex would have considered putting this group of dancers together in a class. Dee was a seasoned waitress, divorced but happy about it, taking the class to stay in shape and become more active. She referred to both Alex and Pedro as 'Honey.' Madison was a student nurse busy with school and determined to maintain her dance skills. She had just broken up with her boyfriend and teased Pedro she was waiting for him to grow up. Pedro was shy and realized the three women were boosting his self-confidence so he would be comfortable performing. He appreciated the attention, but the blunt teasing by the older women often made him blush. Alex also got teased, but he did not blush.

Rosa enrolled in jazz and ballet classes, which meant dancing at least three times a week. She kept in shape and saw Alex often since he taught jazz and tap. She focused on patients and dentistry during the day, but as soon as she finished writing in her last chart, she dreamed of the next time she would see him. At first, she hid in the back row of the jazz class and acted like every other student. But when Alex entered the classroom, he sought her out and gave her a quick, possessive kiss on the lips. He had no intention of hiding their relationship. She was certain she noticed a few disappointed females, but most women smiled at Rosa with approval. Alex was still the taskmaster who expected them to reach their potential, but the class was more relaxed. The women tempered their comments when Pedro joined the group. Because the instructor's girlfriend and a seventeen-year-old boy were taking the class, all talk about Alex and his womanizing ended, and Alex felt comfortable being himself.

***

Life was good for Rosa, but things are never perfect. She had to deal with a strained relationship with her mother and discontent at the house. Chrissy and Mary Lou were at odds. They had never been friends, but they did their best to tolerate each other. After Mary Lou announced her engagement, she was difficult to be around: bragging, and bossy, and constantly complaining about her future in-laws. Rosa and Connie avoided her, but Chrissy found it difficult to ignore the complaints. Chrissy finally lost her patience and told her to shut up. A confrontation occurred when vacationing at the beach house, and an argument between the girls resulted in irreconcilable differences between the roommates. Finally, Mary Lou announced she was moving. She left without notice. The three remaining girls discussed their next move.

"We should take our time looking for a roommate," warned Connie. "We know how miserable it is living in an unhappy household."

Chrissy was upset. "It was my fault; I should have ignored her. Now I will have trouble finding extra rent money, since we will have to cover Mary Lou's portion. All I have is the nanny job."

"I can lend you money for rent as long as it doesn't take too long to find a fourth roommate," offered Rosa. "You might be able to temp through an agency for additional income."

"I can help too," added Connie.

Chrissy burst into tears. "Who am I kidding? My aspirations to model or act are only dreams. I have no real chance; I am a good singer but not good enough, a good actress but not exceptional. The younger girls get the modeling jobs, and I'm ready to pack it in. I gave it my best shot, but maybe I should return to my father in Idaho."

Connie took her hand. "Is there anything else bothering you, Chrissy? What happened at the vacation house? We have no idea what caused the friction."

Chrissy sighed. "Mary Lou overheard Russ calling her a bridezilla after Louis complained about her. She told them off, then Russ left abruptly."

Connie and Rosa couldn't help but smirk at the thought. Mary Lou was a bridezilla.

"So," added Chrissy, "I could tell Russ was upset and didn't want to talk. He apologized and made an excuse about leaving for an emergency job. He probably couldn't wait to wash his hands of the situation. Then I yelled at Mary Lou and told her I was sick of hearing about her wedding."

They regarded Chrissy sympathetically, and then the real problem emerged. The underlying hurt was because of Russ. "He never took me seriously," sobbed Chrissy. "He treated me like a little sister; I tried all the usual signals, and the only thing he did was hold my hand."

Rosa suspected Russ was far more interested than Chrissy realized. "You should understand Russ is older and had reason to believe you didn't want his advances. He offered friendship since he was told you weren't interested in dating anyone."

"That was true at first, but things changed," said Chrissy.

Rosa was sure about Russ and his admiration of Chrissy. "Let him know you want him as a boyfriend. Russ is a great guy but not good at recognizing subtle suggestions. Be blatant." After a pause, Rosa continued. "Of course, it's up to you. But if you start a relationship with him, will you still leave?"

Chrissy shook her head. "It doesn't matter; it's too late. I'm sure the attraction I thought was present exists only in my mind."

Rosa thought Chrissy was making a mistake. "Why don't you call him and find out?"

Chapter 33

It's hard to follow advice. Chrissy, who was normally bold and uninhibited, failed to talk to Russ about her feelings. Rosa understood Chrissy's reluctance; she needed a heart to heart talk with Alex but hesitated. She had dated Alex for months, and the relationship was intimate, yet he failed to discuss his past or family, and had not introduced her to Nana. In contrast, he knew almost everything about Rosa. He worked for her father and met her mother, roommates, boss, dental assistant, and ex-boyfriend. Rosa had been open about her family's secret, but Alex remained a mystery to her. When Alex asked Rosa to attend Mass with Nana and Aunt Mary on Sunday, she finally felt like he was opening up to her. Nana and Aunt Mary were thrilled because Alex had never introduced a girlfriend to them.

Both women thought Rosa was lovely, and Nana recognized the look of love in Alex's eyes. She realized this girl was special. After church, they visited Aunt Mary's house for coffee and cake. Alex asked Rosa if she would attend Mass with them every Sunday, and even though it meant an end to their lazy Sunday mornings, getting to know his family was worth the sacrifice.

Alex was Catholic, and Rosa wondered if he was devout like Nana and Aunt Mary. Rosa felt troubled by the sampler Alex had displayed in his entryway. The Bible passage was haunting. '*The Lord told Eve she would bring forward children in pain, her urge would be for her husband, who would rule over her.*' That was a shocking statement to all women who would pay for Eve's disobedience. She walked over to the sampler.

"Why do you have this, Alex?"

"It is Nana's most exquisite work; she spent months on it after Grandpa died. At the time, we became very close." Then he added, "Nana read the Bible to me as a teenager. Crazy things happened in the Old Testament."

"Do you think there was an apple?" she asked.

"Maybe. More likely, the apple is a metaphor."

"I think so too, Alex. I think the apple is sex."

He gave her a doubtful glance. "Did you go to Catholic school, Rosa?"

"I did."

"What did they teach about the Bible?"

"Not much. They didn't discuss the Old Testament."

"Since I went to public schools, I got my religious training from Nana. I think the apple represents sin. Sex is one of those perplexing realities of life. It is a gift when shared freely as an expression of love. It can be a curse if used to harm or dominate another person. In the early chapters of the Old Testament, they didn't have clear rules; the men sometimes had many wives and concubines. It is hard to relate to those stories today."

"The passage is true," she insisted. "The pain in childbirth is intense; a woman's urge is for her man, and in marriage, the woman vows obedience."

He grasped her hands and offered words of comfort. "Rosa, I hope your urge for me will always be strong, but I promise I'll never rule over you."

Rosa smiled. "Your Nana was a wise teacher, Alex. Because of her, you have a healthy outlook on life and love."

***

Rosa spent every weekend with Alex. She arrived Friday evening for dinner and stayed Saturday morning while he taught at the dance school. Rosa enjoyed time alone in his apartment and tried to make herself useful by cleaning and preparing meals. She doubted Alex used his vacuum, so she brought it out every Saturday. She discovered a box of paperbacks in the hall closet where he stored the vacuum and had fun looking through the selections. Rosa rarely had time to read and thought she would enjoy a novel on Saturday mornings. The books were romances, and the one that caught her attention was about a duke named Alexander. After reading two chapters, she slipped the book into her handbag. She didn't think Alex would mind.

She forgot to mention the book to Alex because she was distracted by his exciting news .

"I might travel to Hollywood for a choreography job. A producer called me and asked for a resume and a video."

"Really? Did you apply for the job?"

"They approached me. A new dance movie will begin production in December. A representative from the studio was in the audience during the showcase and asked Fred Donovan for my contact information. He wants footage of my recent work, and the only videos available were of the Nutcracker and our dances in the showcase."

Rosa's heart dropped, but she managed an encouraging smile. "Sounds like a rare opportunity, Alex. If you get the job, how long will you be in LA?"

"A couple of months at most. It will start in December. This could boost my career and lead to other opportunities in the future."

She was quiet. He sensed a growing tension. "Are you all right, Rosa?"

"Sure. I think it's wonderful, Alex."

"Are you upset about the footage of our dances? Should I ask your permission before I send them?"

"I'm just surprised the dances are on videotape. I don't mind if you send them."

"I should show them to you; we look amazing. The dances were intense and had an impact on the audience. The passionate choreography is just what they want in the movie. Without the performance, they would not have known who I was."

"Congratulations, Alex. I hope you get the job and have success as a choreographer."

Rosa felt like this was the beginning of the end. She always had the dreadful sense that she would only have him for a little while, and the relationship would run its course. Now it seemed his ambition would cause it to end more abruptly. Rosa was attracted to ambitious men, but her career placed limits on her. She could not follow him to Hollywood. He said he would be away for a few months, but this job could lead to other offers in California or other parts of the country. She understood, she was also ambitious. It would be so much easier to love if isolated from the rest of the world. Even Adam and Eve, though living in paradise, had trouble making it work.

Chapter 34

Anita knew she could not mend her relationship with her daughter without providing the details Rosa sought. She did not want to involve her husband, so she drove to Rosa's place for a visit. Rosa knew the intent was to have a heart-to-heart talk, but wanted the encounter to be as pleasant as possible. She introduced Connie and Chrissy, and they all enjoyed getting to know each other as they gathered in the kitchen for coffee and cake. Afterward, Rosa brought her mother to her room for privacy.

"To start, Mom, I want to know who my father is and what happened. Please don't sugarcoat the details. Daddy already told me about your situation and that you and Dad had an arranged marriage."

A deep scar had been left on Anita's heart. After a sigh, she started her story. "My high school sweetheart was Stan Knapik, a Polish boy who was the star of the basketball team. We were an unusual couple; he so tall and quiet, and me, the petite, feisty girl who somehow won his heart. We had an intense summer romance after graduation, and I loved him. In the fall, he left for an out-of-state university on a basketball scholarship. I stayed with my parents and worked as a secretary at an insurance agency. I was desperate to hang on to him and thought if he loved me he would change his plans and go to the community college nearby. But the scholarship is what he had dreamed of for years. We were careless. We used some simple precautions, but were inexperienced and young, and I realized I was pregnant while he was away at school. I didn't have the money to fly out and tell him in person, so I had to do it over the phone. Of course, he was upset. He didn't know what to say, and promised to call me back. I never spoke to him again. That night he veered off the road and died in a car accident. They found alcohol in his system. I never knew whether he planned to take care of me or abandon me, but it didn't matter. I lost him forever. He was an only child and the focus of his family's life. After the funeral, I tried to contact his mother, but Mr. Knapik told me she was too distraught to talk to Stan's friends. After some time passed, I thought it kinder to keep the pregnancy from them. When Oliver offered marriage, the solution seemed simple. You would be legitimate and have a caring father who would love and provide for you."

Both women cried, but Rosa was hesitant to forgive. "You should have told me, Mom. Someday I might be married, and it could be important to know the medical history of my biological father. Don't you think his parents would like to know they have a grandchild?"

"It's not that easy, Rosa. We have lived with this story for so long." Anita slouched and put her hands on her temples. "I'm getting a migraine."

Rosa headed for the door. "You should lie down while I get some aspirin for you." She dimmed the lights and closed the door.

Anita continued to cry and needed a tissue. She opened the nightstand and instead found a pregnancy test. She closed the drawer and imagined history repeating itself. Though upset, she tried to calm herself and imagined Rosa was late and wondering if she was pregnant. She remembered how distraught she had been with her unexpected pregnancy. Anita attempted to approach the subject when Rosa returned.

"Is there anything else you want to talk about, Rosa?"

"No, Mom, I've had enough drama for one night. Please give me information about my grandparents; I want to contact them."

"They have no idea, Rosa. Be gentle. I'm sure it will be a shock."

***

Mr. and Mrs. Knapik lived in town and occupied the same house they had twenty-seven years ago. Rosa wrote a letter of introduction and included her address and phone number. That way, they could contact her when they were ready. She continued to lean on Alex for comfort and support, and he offered to accompany her when she met her grandparents. She savored the hours spent with him since she assumed the relationship would only last until he left for LA in December. The autumn colors were peak when they hiked in the Delaware Water Gap. They enjoyed the glorious autumn in New Jersey and had an overwhelming sense of calm and freedom as they explored the trails. Alex must have kissed her a hundred times that day; he was so animated and enthusiastic. He carried her away with his mood, as Rosa faced the undeniable truth that she had never been so happy. He was the boyfriend she always wanted, a fantasy fulfilled. But the fantasy never extended into marriage. She was twenty-seven years old, and the time had come for adult dreams and plans for the future. She tried to imagine Alex in a more lasting role. Right now, she couldn't do that.

He dropped Rosa off after an exhilarating day. She met Connie in the kitchen. "Rosa, your phone has been ringing all day. I attempted to answer it, but missed the call."

"Oh no. I wonder if it was my grandparents."

When Connie questioned her, she told the story of her biological father. After a long pause, Connie whispered ,"I suspected something was amiss between you and your mother. I knew her visit was not a simple get-together."

"I'm sorry, Connie, I should have told you sooner, but I have trouble talking about it."

They both jumped when the phone rang, and Rosa ran to her room to answer it. The woman spoke softly and hesitantly.

"Hello; I'd like to speak to Rosa Fletcher."

"Speaking."

"Rosa, I'm Helen Knapik. I received your letter and would like to meet you. Would you be able to come to our house sometime this week?"

"I can. What day are you free?"

"We are retired and at home most of the time. Would tomorrow be too soon?"

"Tomorrow is perfect. I can come after work, around 7:30. Would that be convenient?"

"We'll be here. We are looking forward to meeting you."

***

Alex did not have a class that evening, so he picked Rosa up and drove her to her destination. He was happy to go with her and felt his presence would make the meeting easier for all of them. It was not a situation she should face alone. It was possible the grandparents would find it hard to believe they had a granddaughter, or the meeting could be disappointing. Her grandparents were wealthy. The neighborhood was exclusive; the tree-lined lanes were well-manicured, and the Victorian homes were impressive. Alex squeezed her hand as she rang the doorbell. The woman who answered was tall and slim and looked more like Rosa than anyone in her family. In an instant, all doubt disappeared. Her grandmother hugged her tightly and started to cry. Her grandfather joined them. Finally, Alex became part of the group hug.

"We are sorry," whispered her grandfather. "We had no idea we had a granddaughter."

"I just found out too," she replied.

Suddenly, they were all too choked up to talk. Then Alex stepped back. "Hello, I'm Alex ... the boyfriend."

They all smiled and gathered around the kitchen table. Mrs. Knapik served coffee, tea, and a light Polish cookie, a chruściki. Rosa knew nothing about being Polish but sensed her grandparents were proud of their heritage. When they moved to the living room, there was a wall of photographs displaying a handsome young boy and a graduation picture of a young man. "Is this him?" Rosa asked, the tears about to fall at any moment.

"That is Stanley, our only child. We miss him every moment of every day."

"He looks so young." Rosa, filled with a deep sadness, wasn't sure what to say. "I am so sorry for your loss."

"It's your loss too," replied her grandfather.

The visit was draining and bittersweet. They mourned the young man who had died in his youth, the years that had gone by, and the milestones they had missed. Rosa knew her childhood would have been a comfort to them. Anita had made a mistake. Since they were Rosa's family, she would do what she could to make it up to them, maybe provide them with great-grandchildren, and would always include them in her life. The sadness was overwhelming. Alex was charming and upbeat and helped them get through the sentimental visit. Rosa couldn't imagine anyone better suited to guide her through the emotional evening.

Chapter 35

The roommate search left Connie frustrated. She was paying for half the deficit left by Mary Lou's departure, Rosa the other half. Chrissy didn't have the money to chip in. The ad in the local paper attracted unwanted phone calls, mostly from guys with fantasies about living in a house with three women. Inappropriate remarks and suggestive comments made Connie want to change her phone number. Phone sex girls answered these calls for a living; if these losers wanted cheap thrills, they should pay for it. Two women called, but one was a smoker and the other had three cats. Connie kept the smoker's number in case they couldn't find anyone else. Finally, they agreed to meet a college senior looking for a room close to campus. She said she would take the room until her graduation in the spring. When Chrissy answered the door, she liked the girl standing in front of her. She dressed well but casually, and looked pretty with long, curly brown hair and bright blue eyes. She had a friendly, natural smile and looked familiar.

"Hi Megan, I'm Chrissy. You spoke to Connie on the phone; she's waiting in the kitchen."

Megan loved the house and the neighborhood, which was much nicer than expected. The three girls sat down at the kitchen table. Connie asked, "Have we met before, Megan?"

"I don't think so," she replied.

Connie served coffee and tea and tried to make the encounter seem less like an interview. Megan was friendly but shy.

"So, Megan," started Connie, "tell us about yourself. What kind of living space are you looking for?"

"I am a nursing student and had a place near campus, but my housing plans fell through in August. I live with my parents and travel two hours each time I attend classes and hospital rotations. The commute is sometimes longer because of heavy traffic. It would be much easier if I could move closer." She paused and sighed. "I love my parents, but I'm no longer used to living at home."

Both Connie and Chrissy could relate to that. They had a pleasant, candid conversation, and they decided Megan would be a good roommate. Chrissy and Connie showed her the room, which was spacious with a large closet. The rent was reasonable.

"There are no students in the house," noted Chrissy, "but it's quiet during the week, in case you need a place to study."

"My curriculum is mostly clinical, so I won't need the study, just a good night's sleep. One more thing," she cautiously added, "I have a steady boyfriend, and well, we need a place to hang out together."

The girls smiled.

"No problem," they said unanimously.

"If you want the room, you can move in anytime." suggested Connie. "I'm sorry you didn't meet Rosa, our other roommate."

"I already know Rosa. That's how I found out about the vacancy. I'm Russ's sister."

Chrissy turned beet red. Connie was wide-eyed and amused, as things were about to get interesting.

When Rosa returned from her dance class, Connie and Chrissy met her with the news.

Rosa was relieved. "I'm sorry I didn't tell ahead of time, but Megan thought it best you meet her on her own merits. I know Megan. She's sweet, dependable, and an easier person to live with than Mary Lou."

Chrissy had an audition the next day, so she excused herself. She wondered if she would have trouble sleeping with thoughts of encountering Russ. After she left, Rosa sat down with Connie. Rosa needed to talk.

"Are you upset about something?" asked Connie.

"Alex is going to LA in December. He got the job."

"Is he moving?"

"No, he is choreographing dances for a movie. He plans to be back in a few months."

"And that's a problem?"

"Connie, I am emotionally attached to Alex, but did not expect our relationship to last forever. I've been down this road before. Being a dentist means settling in one place, working hard, and restricting time off. Patients depend on you, and it is difficult to find a dentist to take care of emergencies when you are away, especially if you have a solo practice. Alex seems like his future could be in Hollywood, making movies."

"Have you talked to him about it?"

"No, but I can see where this is heading. If he returns to professional dance, he will travel, and if he finds work as a choreographer, he will be away on location. I don't want to rain on his parade, since he seems so happy. I must think about my future."

"I thought you were in love with him, Rosa."

She sighed. "I am. But I don't know if it's a mature love that can withstand the test of time."

"You might break his heart."

"I don't think so. He's resilient and charming, and might appreciate having his freedom back. I don't think he wants to get married, at least not as soon as I want to. Don't worry. I'm sure it won't be an ugly scene. He will go to LA and realize it is time to move on. I will let him go. I'm trying to prepare my heart for the inevitable."

"I hope you know what you're doing, Rosa. Don't act in haste."

Rosa's words were brave, but she couldn't ignore the stabbing pain she felt when she considered life without him. She tried to rationalize that this is what dating is all about. You enjoy time spent with your suitor, but eventually, you need to move forward or move on. Relationships ended or led to marriage. The experience was about making choices and learning. Rosa was unwilling to hang on for years as with Yale. She did not want it to hurt, but of course it would. She picked up the romance novel to escape the thoughts racing in her mind. Duke Alexander and Alex seemed to be the same man, and she wondered if the author had known Alex. When she looked at the copyright, she realized Alex was in grade school when the book first published. Could she trust that Alex is real, or more like a character created for a romance novel? Suddenly, he did not seem like an original, but a man hiding who he was, rarely discussing his emotions, past, or aspirations. Maybe she was star-struck, like she was when reading about a hero in a romance novel. She enjoyed the story, but knew it would end.

***

Alex sensed Rosa was drifting away but did not understand the change in direction. She hid a sadness that seemed to overwhelm her. He wondered if she planned to break up with him before his trip to LA. He knew something was amiss when Oliver called him into his office. If a simple business matter, they would talk at his desk.

"Have a seat, Alex. We need to talk."

"Is there a problem with the audit?"

"No, this is not about work."

Alex dreaded the conversation, though he didn't know what Oliver had on his mind. Oliver glared at him and struggled to remain composed. "Is there something you want to tell me, Alex?"

"I don't think so, sir. Is this about Rosa?"

"It is. Is there something you should tell me?"

"She hasn't been herself lately, but I don't know why."

"So you honestly don't know."

Alex was getting uncomfortable. "Know what?"

Oliver gave him a stern look. "I assume you are having intimate relations with my daughter."

Alex was embarrassed and looked down at his hands. He did not want to talk to Mr. Fletcher about this; he knew Rosa's father disapproved of premarital sex, and Alex couldn't deny it.

"This is what I know, Alex. Anita has been driving me crazy for over a week. She visited Rosa and found a pregnancy test in Rosa's dresser drawer."

Alex turned white, surprised, panicked, and visibly shaken. Finally, he asked, "Did she talk to Rosa?"

"No, Anita hoped you would discuss the situation. She wants to know what is happening, but you seem to know nothing about this."

Mr. Fletcher had a crazy look in his eyes. "I own a shotgun, Alex."

He looked at his boss in disbelief. "You won't have to use it on me, sir, but you might have to use it to persuade your daughter. I don't think she plans to end up with me."

"And why not?"

"I think Rosa wants a professional man. Although we have been happy together, why should she settle for someone like me? Her last boyfriend is on track to be a distinguished cardiac surgeon."

"Her last boyfriend was a schmuck. I thought you were an improvement."

"Thank you, sir."

Both men were at a loss for words. Finally, Alex spoke up. "I don't think Rosa would keep this from me; we are merely speculating. Was the test used? Was it positive?"

"Anita didn't know what she was looking at. She did not know there were home pregnancy tests. She thought you needed a blood test at the doctor's office."

Alex tried to calm himself. "We need to hear it from Rosa. All I can say is you can count on me, Mr. Fletcher. I don't want to do anything to hurt your daughter."

Oliver looked at Alex and finally decided to address the issue haunting him. "I like you, Alex, but I don't understand you. You are smart, and charismatic, and have been an excellent employee. But you graduated several years ago and seem to have no clear direction. What do you want to do with your life? You seem unsettled and unprepared to be a husband or a father. I suppose Anita and I will have to accept you if you have fathered our grandchild. But what are you planning to do?"

Alex didn't respond. He did not know how to reassure Rosa's father because everything Oliver said was true. Finally, he resorted to the only honest answer he could give. "Mr. Fletcher, all I want to do is make your daughter happy, and I'm good at it. I have always adapted to whatever life throws at me. I hope that everything else will fall into place."

***

Carl was coming over that night with Lawrence. Alex offered to pay Lawrence to take care of the birds while he was in LA. Both birds had become chatty, and after Carl observed them, he had a suggestion for Alex. "Cleo is looking around Al. I think you should put the nesting box in with them. You don't want eggs at the bottom of the cage."

Alex looked pale. "Do you think there will be eggs?"

"I think it's inevitable. They have been quite active and seem to have an affinity for each other. Because Cleo is young, she might start with eggs that don't hatch."

"I won't be here, Carl. I'll probably be in LA."

"Perhaps it is for the best; you seem so worried. Parakeets reproduce in the wild without our help. The process is not a big deal like it is with us humans. Nature takes care of them and their young."

"I trust your judgment, Carl. I suppose you see this all the time at the shop."

"I do, Al, though I rarely see birds that like each other as much as these two."

Chapter 36

The next time Alex saw Rosa was at Tap. The class was fun, but she seemed distant. Alex was becoming unsettled and convinced that Mr. Fletcher was right. After a troubled sleep, he looked into the nesting box. An egg. '*Oh God, it's true,*' he thought. He had a sense of living in a parallel universe with Buster. Filled with apprehension and overcoming a lack of sleep, he dragged himself to the accounting office. He didn't get work done, but because Oliver was back, it didn't matter. Alex wondered if Mr. Fletcher could sleep at night; he couldn't, and he needed solitude to think. He needed a beer. Getting drunk would not solve his problems, but it might help him deal with the shock. He planned to buy a six-pack at a local store, but after entering the premises he noticed Yale. Alex tried to avoid him, but couldn't.

"So, Albert, how are you? You look terrible."

"Thanks, Yale. What are you doing in town?"

He held up a bottle of expensive champagne. "I thought Rosa might like to celebrate my promotion. It seems like I will continue to practice cardiology in New York."

"Are you going out with her?"

"I called, and we are meeting tonight. Are you going out with her?"

"We're getting married," he blurted. He regretted his statement, but couldn't undo it.

"Liar. In your dreams, Albert."

Yale's gaze seemed to burrow into Alex's soul. He was uneasy. "The only reason she would consider you is if she were knocked up."

Alex remained stone-faced, but Yale picked up on the look of panic in his eyes. Yale was furious. "Should I kill you now, or later?"

"Calm down, Yale, I didn't say anything." Alex left the six-pack on the counter. He would buy beer at another store and talk to Rosa immediately, since he could no longer live with uncertainty. He tried calling her at work, but she had left for the day, and there was no answer at home. She did not come over to his place on Friday night. He stumbled through his Saturday morning dance classes, realizing she was avoiding him. He wondered if this was the end.

***

He had already committed to the movie but would change plans if Rosa needed him. His students were told that Jackie would take over his dance classes until he returned. Oliver was negotiating with a young CPA interested in a partnership, and Mr. Diaz was planning to work until a partner was in place. Everyone was prepared for Alex's departure. He had no reason to stay in New Jersey unless Rosa was in trouble. After many unsuccessful attempts to contact Rosa, he was ready to give up. He was just as upset with her as she was with him, but he needed to make sure she wasn't pregnant. He wouldn't abandon her. She finally answered the phone.

"Alex?"

"Hi, Rosa."

There was a long silence. She had a quiver in her voice. "You don't have to worry about my being pregnant, Alex. I'm not."

That gave him some relief. Then she added, "So you won't have to marry me."

The disdain shocked him. He tried to explain, "No, Rosa, I think you misunderstand."

"I understand Alex. I don't want to talk to you. That was a bizarre thing you did, telling Yale I was pregnant, and that we were getting married."

"I never told him you were pregnant."

"You implied. The last thing I want to do is coerce a man into marriage. Your actions are too outrageous, Alex; I don't think I can trust you."

"And what about you, Rosa? You're the one having dinner with your ex-boyfriend and social outings with your boss."

"You misunderstand. With Yale, I was celebrating a promotion with a friend, and Gerry is not a threat; he's gay."

"Rosa, you're so naïve. Yale wants you back in his bed, and Gerry is not as gay as you think he is. I witnessed your dancing with him. There is a mutual attraction."

"You don't know Gerry."

"I have been dancing for a long time, and I can recognize the sexual tension between partners. I am sure Gerry likes women too."

Another long pause allowed him to clarify his point. "It should be simple, Rosa. You could have told Yale you were happy about his promotion but couldn't go out with him because you were dating me. Gerry would have understood if you told him your boyfriend was uncomfortable and you would like to keep the relationship professional. Instead, you chose to hurt my feelings to spare theirs."

"You are too possessive, Alex. I thought you were more sophisticated than that."

"I'm not difficult to figure out, Rosa. I am a normal male who does not want to see his woman involved with other men. I joke around with the ladies at work but have no intention of bedding them. It is no joke that both Yale and Gerry want you for themselves."

She was silent. It seemed she was giving him the last word, so he took it. "Don't call me back, Rosa, unless you are ready to take me seriously. I don't regret our time together, but if we can't go any further, there's no point in continuing. As your friend, I'll leave you with this advice. If you choose between your two wealthy, successful doctors, pick Gerry. I'm sure Yale would make a miserable husband."

Gently, he put the phone down. She heard a soft click at the other end. It was over.

Chapter 37

Megan moved the last weekend in October. She transported clothes in her car and asked Russ to bring the furniture in his van. He was away attending a friend's wedding that weekend but promised to haul the furniture during the week. She was adamant about settling in by November 1st; she was already staying at the house, sleeping on the couch, ready to move in and organize her bedroom. Finally, she asked Russ to bring her furniture on Halloween night.

"Are you busy tonight, Russ?"

"No, my trick-or-treating days are over."

"I plan to leave for a party by 8 o'clock and need to move the furniture before my ride gets here. I would like you here by dinnertime. Could you bring your tools and look at the upstairs shower? The water pressure is low, like showering with a garden hose."

"Anything else?" he asked sarcastically. She demanded these things before November 1st, and he indulged her. He didn't want to drive on Halloween with all the pedestrian traffic, but he was a doting brother and agreed. Megan helped him move the furniture, then left for the party. The showerhead was beyond repair. He walked to his van to see if he had a replacement. Chrissy was at the door, handing out candy to the neighborhood kids. Her roommates were all out for the evening, and Russ worried it wasn't safe for Chrissy to be alone while answering the door. He found things to repair in the bathroom until she turned the porch lights off at 8:30. The neighborhood was quiet. When he walked to the kitchen to get a glass of water, Chrissy was in the family room watching '*Halloween*', a horror movie about girls murdered while babysitting. He was upset.

"Chrissy, I can't believe you're alone watching this movie."

"I'm not alone," she whispered. She smiled and made room for him on the couch. He sat next to her, but did not want to watch the movie. Instead, he watched Chrissy.

"You're not going to let me watch the movie, are you?" she asked, exasperated. She turned the TV off and looked at Russ. "Now you'll have to talk to me."

He was upset by the hostility in her voice. "What's bothering you, Chrissy?"

"Why didn't you call me, Russ?"

"I didn't think you wanted me to. I wanted to be with you, but felt I was getting in the way."

"I can't believe you took what Mary Lou said to heart. She's a witch."

Russ was flustered, and he needed a moment to compose himself. He returned to the kitchen for more water.

"Help yourself to a beer," she suggested. "There's leftover candy on the table."

He returned and sat down. Chrissy remembered that Rosa had told her to be blunt. "Aren't you even slightly attracted to me, Russ?"

He couldn't believe her question. He had never been so attracted to a woman in his life. He confessed. "Chrissy, I'm so attracted to you that I had to stop seeing you. I found it difficult to be your friend because of it. I sensed you were vulnerable and didn't want to take advantage."

"Last summer I was looking for friendship," she admitted, "but now I want more."

He was so overwhelmed with emotion that he couldn't say anything. He took her into his arms, and finally they kissed. Chrissy was not the innocent young girl he imagined her to be. She was a passionate woman, ready to accept the attention he dreamt of giving her. They both realized they were about to take it all the way. "My roommates will be home soon," she whispered. "Let's go to my room."

Megan had too much to drink at the party. When she walked upstairs, she heard Russ whispering in Chrissy's room. Megan knew what was happening. She tiptoed down the stairs and headed for the kitchen. Connie and Charlie were eating candy and drinking beer.

"How was your party?"

"Good," she replied, but seemed distracted.

Then Connie asked, "Did Russ fix the shower?"

"I don't know; he's not working on it now. He's in Chrissy's room."

Charlie smiled and looked down at the table. He knew Russ had been waiting for Chrissy all summer.

"Don't worry, Megan," said Connie. "This is not a reckless fling. They have suppressed a longing for each other since the beginning of the summer. I guess they finally did something about it."

***

Alex continued to prepare for his trip to LA. He put in extra hours at the accounting office. Mr. Fletcher was sorry Rosa broke up with Alex but did not say anything; he did not want to interfere again. Alex received the movie script along with the music for the dances, so he stayed up late reading through the dialogue. He was interested in the main characters and hoped they would consider his casting suggestions. Work helped distract him from the heartache of missing Rosa. He could not take back what he said on the phone, but needed to express his true feelings. He had not heard from her, but realized he should not be the one to make a move since he left her with the choice to move forward or end the relationship.

Alex planned to spend Thanksgiving with family and friends before leaving. This year, Tammy was preparing the feast but served dinner in Alex's apartment since his living room was large and the guests would not have to navigate the stairs. All three kitchens were being used; the turkey was cooking in the basement oven, Tammy's mom had pies in Alex's kitchen, and everything else was upstairs with Tammy and Carl. Alex set the table with Nana's china, and Lawrence was there to help. Tammy had never prepared a Thanksgiving dinner and wanted everything to be perfect. This was the first holiday Tammy and Carl hosted as an engaged couple. They were getting married in the summer, and their guests were excited about the upcoming nuptials. Carl brought fun and laughter into Tammy's life, and Mrs. Lewis could see the positive change in her daughter and grandson. He was dressed like a gentleman but still looked like a biker. Though Carl had a new interest in his appearance, he was a big guy with tattoos regardless of what he wore. Tammy brought out a platter after Carl carved the turkey. The feast was about to begin.

"I don't know why we didn't do a turkey breast," she complained. "Everyone likes white meat."

Carl took Tammy's hand. "Well," he whispered, "I prefer dark meat."

She slapped him on the shoulder. Carl was acting naughty in front of her mom, Nana, and Aunt Mary. But the three women giggled, and then everyone laughed. Carl was proud of Tammy, and their affinity for each other was undeniable. Even Tammy's church group approved of Carl. They thought having Carl in attendance made the group seem more inclusive.

Russ and Chrissy joined the gathering for dessert. Chrissy was stunning in a long flowered skirt and peasant blouse. Her hair was straight and simple, and she wore very little makeup. She was a natural beauty. Chrissy followed Alex into the kitchen as he was washing the china. She stood beside him, put her hand over his, and looked at him with concern.

"How are you, Alex?"

"I'm sad, Chrissy."He didn't plan to ask, but since they were alone, he took the opportunity. "How is Rosa?"

Chrissy sighed. "Her room is next to mine, and I hear her crying at night." The comment made the heartbreak worse. Then she asked, "What happened?"

"You know, Chrissy, I'm not sure."

Chrissy felt terrible. She knew he was hurting too.

"Can I give you a bit of advice, Chrissy?"

"Sure."

"If Russ does something to upset you, just talk to him. Chances are he won't even realize you're mad. Always talk about it, and never give him the silent treatment. It never works well."

"I know Alex. We wasted the summer misunderstanding each other. It won't happen again."

After an upbeat performance all day, Alex allowed a rare moment of self-pity. He thought about the couples together because of him: Chrissy and Russ, Carl and Tammy, Cleo and Buster. Even Aunt Mary and Nana were together because Nana wanted him to have the house. But for him, loneliness. He no longer had Russ or Carl to share in his misery. He was glad he was leaving because he didn't want to subject them to his depression.

Rosa was always restless on Thanksgiving night. She didn't know if it was due to overeating or if the turkey upset her stomach. She was in her old room at the lake and woke up twice with the same haunting dream. She was in the ocean with Alex, but a gigantic wave swept him away. She struggled to find him. She was on the beach, crying for help, but no one would assist her. After waking up a second time, she realized the nightmare was telling her something. It was up to her to get him if she wanted him back.

Chapter 38

Rosa's window of opportunity to reconcile passed when Alex flew to LA. She experienced a sense of regret, but he was ambitious, and she didn't want to tie him down. Settling down was not in his immediate future. Alex had not talked about love or commitment, and she had to remember him for what he was to her: the most wonderful boyfriend she had, and she would never forget their time together. Dawn sensed Rosa's melancholy and asked about Alex.

"I broke up with him, Dawn."

"Why did you do that?"

"It's complicated."

Dawn crossed her arms over her chest and glared at her. "Dr. Fletcher, it's not that complicated. He's crazy about you. I'll never forget when he knelt in the waiting room helping you with those ballroom shoes. It was like Cinderella and her prince."

"Life is not a fairy tale. He's in LA."

"Well, go get him."

Dawn made it sound so simple. Rosa had made a mistake. She avoided him, and that was the worst thing she could do. She could have expressed her concerns, and even if the outcome was the same, at least they would have discussed it. This way, the relationship remained unfinished – and might never be resolved. Rosa realized he also had insecurities, but she had done little to support him; she was just like Yale, accepting his effort in the relationship as though entitled. She had not asked him what he wanted because she was afraid of the answer. It was the last month of an emotional year. She braced herself for the third depressing Christmas in a row. When Yale asked her out for New Year's Eve, she agreed. The party was in Manhattan, at an exclusive ballroom, close enough to Times Square to watch the ball drop. A popular band would perform, and the event was to be televised. It was an exciting opportunity to experience the New Year in New York.

She bought a dress for the occasion that was sophisticated, glamorous, and sexy. Finally, she had the money to buy classy outfits regardless of price. Rosa perfected her hair and makeup. She was confident, professional, in her prime, and at the perfect age to attract someone special and settle down. Chrissy knocked on her door to wish her a happy new year. Chrissy was planning to spend the night with Russ.

"Rosa, you look fabulous. I hope you know what you're doing. Yale will be all over you tonight."

Rosa once again studied her image in the mirror. The dress was revealing, short, and showcased her beautiful shape. "Should I change?"

"Hell no, you look marvelous, but don't be surprised if he comes on to you. He doesn't seem like the type who controls himself."

"I want him to know I have changed and am not the same accommodating girl I used to be. I doubt he expects me to spend the night. We're not dating anymore."

Chrissy gave her a doubtful look. Rosa could be clueless.

When Yale picked her up, he was dashing in his dark grey suit and exhibited a maturity and polish she found impressive. The evening was full of excitement. Many of Yale's colleagues attended the party with their wives and girlfriends. Rosa enjoyed meeting interesting people, and though they avoided the dance floor, she had a wonderful time. As midnight approached, Yale led her outside so he could be alone with her.

The ball was about to drop. He turned to her. "Rosa, I hope this is a new beginning for us." He took her into his arms and kissed her. She allowed it but stiffened.

"Are you cold?" he asked.

"Maybe," she replied. "Let's go inside."

He brought her onto the dance floor. The music was slow, and his hands slid to her lower back as he pulled her in. She felt him pressed against her and realized he expected her in his bed. He had too much to drink. She pulled away. He looked at her curiously.

"Talk to me, Rosa."

"I'm sorry, Yale. This doesn't feel right."

"Rosa, I expect you to come to my apartment tonight. We're not strangers; we had six years of intimacy. I assure you I can get you in the mood. You are going to spend the night with me."

"I won't, Yale. You're moving too fast, and I can't turn it on and off that easily."

"You could have fooled me. I thought the outfit was an invitation. After your string of boyfriends, I assumed you wouldn't be such a prude."

"It's like you to blame my dress for your behavior."

"I never thought you were a tease. Why did you go out with me?"

"You were persistent, and I thought you cared. I didn't think you would pressure me."

"There are women who would love to spend New Year's Eve with me. I thought it wouldn't be such a big deal since we're so well acquainted."

"If I remember correctly, Yale, you said I was a disappointment and told me I wasn't very good at it. That was quite rich since you were the only man I had been with and did everything you asked to please you. It's not the type of thing a girl forgets."

"That's ridiculous. Why would I stay with you for years if I wasn't happy with our sex life?"

"Maybe you needed someone to be there for you. I suspect there were others."

"And what about you? Are you still screwing your dance instructor? "

She was furious, but nodded no. He calmed down and spoke more softly. "What's the problem?"

She sighed. "We're not right for each other, and I'm not in love with you. I should go home."

"Good luck. Either come home with me or find a way back to New Jersey. I'm in no condition to drive."

He turned and left her alone at their table. Rosa was ready to burst into tears. She was drunk and alone in New York City and wondered if she had enough cab fare to get to her house. Yale should have recognized the lack of chemistry that was a persistent issue in their relationship. He hadn't been able to get the response he expected from her, not tonight or during the six years they had dated. Just then, Gerry appeared.

"Happy New Year, Rosa." They hugged.

"Gerry, have you been here all night?"

"Yes, I saw you but didn't want to interrupt your date."

He turned toward the bar. Yale was talking to the female bartender. "Do you need a ride home?"

"I do. You're a lifesaver, Gerry. Are you here with someone?"

"No, I came alone and met friends here. I can leave anytime."

"How about now?" she asked

"That's fine, Rosa. I've never been a fan of New Year's Eve; 1983 was a tough year." Then he asked, "Do you want Yale to see us leaving together?"

"Yes, Gerry, if you don't mind. I'm sorry to get you involved, but he should know I have a ride home, and seeing us together might end his persistence."

Gerry put his arm around her. "You don't have to look; I'll make sure he sees us walking out."

Yale took one last look at Rosa. He didn't understand why he continued to pursue her; then he realized her feelings for him had been pure and honest. She didn't care about his wealth or prestigious career. She wanted him, and he missed his chance to be with a woman who loved him for himself. He was unfaithful while they were dating, and she became suspicious. It was impossible to regain her trust, and in his heart, he knew he didn't deserve it.

On the drive home, Gerry and Rosa talked about their personal lives. Gerry was leaving the geriatric hospital and planned to move out of state. He accepted a position as an administrator at a teaching hospital in the Midwest. The facility had a program dedicated to AIDS research. He was concerned about the staff he was leaving behind and the longevity of the programs he had started. He asked Rosa about her intentions.

"Rosa, do you plan to continue your work at the dental clinic?"

"I will stay for a while, but not long-term. There's no money in it, Gerry. The clinic may attract a new dentist who needs experience or a semi-retired dentist who wants to continue caring for patients. But unless the employment agreement changes, you will not get a dentist to commit."

"I won't be here much longer, Rosa. Will you stay until they hire your replacement?"

"If the new administrator wants me to, I can help. I will miss Dottie, and I will miss you."

Gerry walked her to her doorstep. The evening was chilly, with snowflakes dancing around them. They held on to each other in the cold night and continued to embrace. He felt warm, comfortable, and familiar, and he was leaning, wanting. She looked at him curiously. Then he confessed.

"I wasn't honest with you at the Christmas party last year. I wished I could act on my feelings and the attraction I felt. But I was living with Art and was concerned that I might be harboring the deadly virus that was making my friends sick. There was no way I could act on my interest, but you awakened feelings I didn't realize I had. The truth is, I miss being with a woman. I thought I was gay because I was in love with my college roommate, but before I met him, I never questioned my sexuality. My life hasn't been the same since. He was into the whole gay scene, and I wasn't, and because I valued monogamy, we didn't continue the relationship. He died last summer, and I realized my lifestyle was more about him than about being gay. I'm not running away, Rosa, but getting a fresh start in a place where I am needed."

She allowed him to remain close. "Are you healthy, Gerry?"

"They tell me I am, but I will wait longer to make sure I am safe to be with. I have seen so much sickness and tragedy, I am inclined to be extremely careful about the future. The next person will be a lifelong commitment, a traditional marriage. I hope I can find a woman who can accept my past."

She cared about him and wanted to assure him that her feelings had been mutual. "You will find a woman who will have you, that is for sure. We might have had a chance, but the timing wasn't right."

"I thought so too, but then I saw you dancing with Alex and assumed you would end up together. What happened?"

" Life, careers, and people tend to get in the way. It still hurts."

"Well, Rosa, we will part as friends. I am open to a romantic relationship in the future if we are both unattached and still thinking of each other, but we would have a long-distance problem to deal with. The friendship will always be there."

"It will, Gerry. And so will the attraction."

Rosa felt a little heartache when she considered what might have been. Gerry was the nicest guy she had ever known. She rushed to her room and closed the door behind her. Rosa felt so lonely. It was only a few hours into 1984. Already it sucked.

Chapter 39

Gerry started his tenure as the CEO of a top research facility in the Midwest. They hired a new administrator at the geriatric hospital who intended to move funding for dental services to other aspects of patient care. Without Dr. Ryan, the clinic's longevity was in question. The job lost much of its appeal for Rosa, and she gave her notice. She would miss working with Dottie, but the job had no future, and she was tired of dealing with Medicaid.

Rosa continued working at Dental Connections. She was now more experienced and productive, and working three days per week and an occasional Saturday resulted in an income she could live with. She decided she could afford to remain part-time. Rosa had a following; new patients would request her, and regular patients had become more consistent. They appreciated her kind and diplomatic approach to their dental problems.

A young college guy in for his six-month cleaning had gingivitis, which had not cleared up despite home care instructions. In a very nice way, Rosa gave him advice about brushing and flossing during his first checkup. On this second appointment, she approached the problem more forcefully.

"Robert, have you been able to floss every night?"

He burst out laughing. "Doc, I'm so busy at school I'm lucky if I remember to brush."

She looked so disappointed as he added, "But I promise I will try harder."

Dr. Fletcher acknowledged his promise but added, "My dental school mentor suggested that patients only floss the teeth they want to keep."

He laughed again. "Point taken, Doc. How did you know I wasn't flossing?"

"I just know," she replied.

"Well, it's a good thing I was honest."

She admired him; an honest man. Every man in her life had been deceptive – Yale, Gerry, Alex, even her dad. They all had their reasons, but their duplicity made her less trusting. That night, Rosa re-read the romance novel about Duke Alexander. She doubted she would have the chance to return it and was embarrassed she had taken it from Alex's closet. She understood why this story resonated with Alex. Duke Alexander grew up under unusual circumstances, a boy reared by an older female relative. When the duke discovered he was an earl and inherited a fortune, he had to reinvent himself to be accepted by the ton. He grew up surrounded by women and learned to appreciate them; he was comfortable having lively conversations with them, and the other gentlemen whispered about his tendencies. They failed to value the female intellect and used women for housekeeping and childbearing. Most of their conversations were with other men discussing business, card games, or horses. The only way Alexander could explain his rapport with the opposite sex was to present himself as a womanizer, a rake. The ladies thought he was delightful; they enjoyed the constant banter and teasing. They knew he was all talk and found they could flirt with him and he would not take it seriously. The men imagined him having affairs with many women, especially those who were older or widowed. He had a reputation, but it was based on a lie. Like Alex. *'Oh God,'* she thought, 'H*e never gave me a reason not to trust him.'* The truth is his eye never wandered while he was with Rosa, and she somehow knew he was faithful when interacting with his female colleagues.

Rosa didn't feel like socializing. She spent most of her free time reading or visiting her parents and grandparents. When she went to dinner with her grandparents on Valentine's Day; she suspected they were trying to cheer her up. Rosa wore sweatpants all weekend and rarely went out; she joined a gym, but that was her only activity. On a typical Saturday night, Rosa was in her pajamas. She planned to read 'The Life of Doc Holliday', a historical fiction novel she started about America's most notorious dentist. She was ready to sink into her pillows and read until she was too tired to continue. A knock on her door interrupted her plans; it was Chrissy. She was crying.

"Russ and I had a fight," she sobbed.

"What happened?"

"I can't talk about it, Rosa; I'm mad at him. I need to get out of the house. He will call, and I don't want to be here to answer."

"Maybe you should talk to him, Chrissy."

"No, if I talk to him now, I'll lash out and we'll break up for good. It's best to wait." Valiantly, she tried to gain control of her voice. "Will you go out with me, Rosa?"

"Oh, Chrissy, I don't think it's a good idea; you might do something rash, and I'm already in my pajamas."

"Well, I'll go by myself then. I'm sorry I bothered you."

Rosa followed her into the hallway. "If you're determined, I will go with you. Give me a few minutes to get dressed."

Chrissy had her leopard jumpsuit on, and that meant trouble. Rosa combed her hair, applied light-colored lip gloss, and slipped on her favorite black dress. Chrissy was waiting for her at the front door. "Let's take my car, Rosa. I need to fill up at the gas station."

Chrissy drove to Mother's Pub. Rosa didn't object; it was close, and Chrissy would have friends there. They sat at the bar and ordered frozen margaritas. Chrissy downed the drink in less than five minutes.

"Do you have a brain freeze?" asked Rosa.

"No, but I need to use the ladies' room. Save my seat."

Rosa smiled at the bartender as she sipped her margarita. He was hustling on Saturday night, and the bar was getting crowded.

And then, like a rush of cold air, she felt a thrill pass through her entire being. She sensed him before she saw him. He had his hand on the back of her chair. When she turned, she was in awe of him. He was so incredibly sexy.

"Can I buy you a drink?" he asked.

She gazed into his dreamy blue eyes. "I already have a drink," she replied, but asked, "Can I buy you a drink?"

"Ok." He sat down on the empty bar stool.

"What would you like?"

"I'll have what you're having."

She couldn't help but notice he was looking at her legs.

"That dress is incredible," he whispered as he looked her over.

Suddenly, she had an overwhelming sense of relief and gave him a sultry smile. "I'm glad you like it because I like you."

Rosa and Alex couldn't stop smiling. After a seductive pause, he added, "I like you too, Rosa."

The music was blasting *'Steal Away'* by Bobbie Dupree. She leaned into him. "I'd like to talk to you, but I can't hear."

He gave her a dashing smile. "Your place or mine?"

"Which is closer?"

"I imagine mine is since I walked."

Rosa looked around for Chrissy. "Alex, I have to find Chrissy."

"I'm sure she's not here, Rosa."

"How would you know?"

"Because I came with Russ, who has also disappeared. I'm pretty sure we've been set up."

Rosa didn't believe it. "No, Alex, Chrissy argued with Russ and wanted to go out to forget about it."

Alex chuckled. "I heard a similar story, only there were two problems. One, Russ is a terrible liar, and two, he's even a worse actor."

They put on their coats and ventured into the cold March wind. Chrissy's car was no longer in its parking spot. "I think Chrissy deserves an Academy Award for that performance. I guess she was sure you wouldn't leave me here." He put his arm around her as they walked to his house. They strolled in silence, both wondering what to say. She had missed him and was grateful to be on his front steps. The soft lights were on as they entered the living room.

"Can I get you a drink?" he asked.

She followed him to the kitchen. "Sure."

"I'm sorry, I don't have ginger ale."

"Do you have something stronger?"

"Tequila?"

Although hesitant, she said yes. Rosa watched him pour two shots along with salt and lime. "Have you done this before?"

"No."

"Well, just follow what I do."

The tequila felt like liquid fire to Rosa, but it was the lime she complained about. "That lime could take the enamel right off your teeth."

He hesitated. "Would you like another?"

"Ok."

After the second shot, there was no hesitation. "Do you want to talk?" he asked.

She grabbed his shirt and pulled him to her. "I don't want to talk, Alex."

He pulled her even closer. "Neither do I."

His searing kisses pulled her in, and she could feel he was desperate for her. It was agonizingly hot, with no space between them. Rosa used her body to encourage him; there was no longer an emotional barrier; the past hurt, forgiven. They responded to the visceral pull; with fire in their veins and longing in their hearts, there was a sense of absolute connection. His touch was familiar, but her appreciation of him heightened. As the sizzling tension built, she begged him to make love to her. He pulled her dress down to her waist and continued to seduce her. She left the dress there but removed her underwear. He pressed her against the kitchen counter, a desperate man. Her urgency encouraged him. He wanted her desperately, realizing it was the most primal, lustful moment of his life. She put her hand on his chest, his shirt open, and felt his banging heart. He moved to her and savored this epic return to the woman he belonged to. They kissed passionately, but the need was so great they skipped all preliminaries and immediately addressed their overwhelming desires. When she started to climax, he abandoned tenderness and took her without restraint. He continued to indulge until she went somewhere beyond ecstasy. She had tears in her eyes and found it hard to breathe as he buried himself deep inside her and poured himself into her. They were lightheaded; their climax was extraordinary and shocking.

"Bloody hell, Rosa, what just happened?"

"I don't know, but I thought I was going to die."

"Do you think we could do it again?"

"Maybe. I never imagined being so fiery hot, and explosive. I feel faint."

He had a tight grip on her; she was trembling and felt limp in his arms. The way Rosa responded to him was thrilling, but his remark was teasing. "I tried to warn you about the kitchen."

Rosa felt surprised at how wildly she responded to him. They were drenched in each other and unwilling to move; the connection was too intense to let go. Alex gazed at her. She was radiant in the afterglow of their lovemaking, her eyes stormy and ever-changing. Alex, mesmerized, felt a connection to her soul. Finally, he composed himself and gave her a hopeful smile. "Can I assume you missed me?"

She wondered if her boldness and aggression shocked him, and imagined she looked as wild as she felt. "Of course I missed you." Then she couldn't suppress her grin. "Bloody hell?"

He assumed she would tease him for that. "I know you have the book, Rosa."

"What makes you think I have your book?"

"There are only three people who enter my apartment unsupervised; Carl, who asked to borrow books, and that is when I discovered "*Duke Alexander'* was missing; Lawrence, who undoubtedly would come to me with questions about the book, and you. 'Bloody hell' is a common swear phrase in historical romance novels."

She laughed. "Oh, Alex," she beamed, "I love you."

His look turned serious. "Do you?"

She became serious too. "I do."

"Well then, that's perfect," he said, "because I love you too."

The truth revealed itself naturally, as it should. Rosa wondered why it took months of separation to verbalize it. She looked over at the birds. "They saw everything, Alex."

"And how does that make you feel?"

She blushed. "It made me feel hot," she admitted. "I will forever feel flushed when in this kitchen."

Gently, he left her but continued to hold her close. He examined the birds in their cage. "What if our pets could be novelists or playwrights? Imagine the stories they could tell." He gazed at her with longing in his eyes. "Will you sleep in my bed tonight?"

"That depends," she answered. "Do you still have the fluffy feather pillows?"

"I do."

"How about the soft white quilt?"

"It's turned down and waiting."

"I'll stay as long as you want."

"Always."

He joined her in the bedroom after he had placed the blanket over the birdcage. He wooed her until the early morning sunlight started peeking through his window. They slept, exhausted but happy. At 7 am his internal clock woke him, and he sat upright.

" Alex?"

"I promised to take Nana and Aunt Mary to 8 am Mass. You can stay here and sleep in."

"I want to go with you, Alex, but I'll have to wear my black dress. It's inappropriate for church."

"You can keep your coat on."

"What if Aunt Mary asks us over? I'm sure she will."

"Get dressed, Rosa; I have an idea."

Alex reached into the back of his closet and gave her a hand-crocheted sweater. "Aunt Mary made this for me. It's warm and comfy, but she must have imagined I was in the NBA. Look at how long it is."

Rosa tried it on, and it covered most of her dress. An inch of black lace showed beyond the hemline. "This is perfect, Alex. It's soft and cozy, and though big, it is attractive. I might have to steal this from you."

He took her hand and whispered. "Whatever I have is yours."

***

Seeing Rosa waiting in the car surprised Nana and Aunt Mary. They were relieved at the apparent reconciliation. When he returned from LA, Alex seemed depressed, and they were worried about his broken heart. Nana remembered being young and single; so wonderful but confusing and traumatic. She sensed he had his heart set on Rosa, but just because he wanted her didn't mean they would end up together. She realized that the reconciliation was new and fragile. Nana steered away from personal inquiries and asked Alex about his business ventures.

"I finally signed the contract, and we have a deal," he said proudly. "I am now part owner of Donovan Dance Studio."

"Are you going into business here?" asked Rosa.

"I didn't discuss it just in case Fred and Jackie changed their minds, but yes, I will eventually buy them out. They plan to retire in Florida in a few years and gave me the first option to buy. I made what I thought was a fair offer, and they accepted it. I truly think they wanted me to take over regardless of price."

"Then why make the trip to LA?"

"I needed money for the down payment. The movie job paid well and was a great experience."

"This is so exciting," said Aunt Mary. "I believe you will be even more successful than the Donovans. You have a background in accounting and business."

Alex thought she was right. Fred was not a good businessman; Jackie was the one who kept the business going for so many years.

Rosa was stunned by the conversation. "I thought you wanted to be a choreographer."

"I will choreograph at the studio every day. The movie job was great, but how many dance movies do they make? I'm more likely to choreograph for Broadway, and living in northern New Jersey is perfect. Besides, I am not interested in fame. For me, it's all about creating and enjoying. I don't want it to consume my life."

He had a point. It was clear to Rosa he wasn't going anywhere, and though very talented, he wouldn't leave his home to advance his career.

When they said goodbye, Nana hugged her. She had tears in her eyes. "I am so happy to see you, Rosa. You know, Alex means the world to us."

Rosa knew how much Nana and Aunt Mary loved Alex and appreciated their approval. As they drove back to his house, Alex hoped to nap and relax with Rosa in his arms. But first, he realized, they needed to talk.

Chapter 40

" I have to get out of this dress," she complained as she kicked off her heels.

"Ok." He smiled and waited.

"I hope you can find something for me to wear."

"All right." He gave her a t-shirt and gym shorts, comfy but he could still admire her legs. They sat in the living room. "My mother told me what happened," started Rosa. "She found the pregnancy test and insisted my father confront you. I understand why you had the wrong idea when you ran into Yale."

"I felt protective," confessed Alex, "and was upset because of your father."

"I bet that was an interesting conversation."

"He loves you, Rosa. And though he likes me, I suspect he wanted to beat me up."

There was a long silence. Then disarmed, he spoke of his true feelings. " I assumed your relationship with Yale was over, and that you decided to be with me. It hurt to hear you were seeing him again."

Rosa was emotional, and the lack of sleep nullified any attempt at self-control. "You were leaving," she sobbed. "I thought you were done with me and it was time to move on."

"Seeing Yale wasn't moving on."

"I realize that now. But Alex, you didn't discuss your plans with me, and I assumed you were making a big debut in Hollywood."

"That only happens in the movies. My life is here, and I have no desire to roam around the country. I did that when I was in the dance company. Besides, I have my house to take care of."

"You own the house?"

"I do. Nana signed it over to me when I turned eighteen."

"What are your intentions, Alex?"

"To run the dance studio as long as I enjoy it and it is profitable. I took the job in California for the money and to make valuable contacts for the future. I am not intent on fame, Rosa. I want to create, teach, and spend time with you. I hoped to continue our relationship when I returned and expected it to be exclusive."

"Is that what you want, Alex?"

"It is."

She snuggled against him and ran her fingers through his blond curls; she knew that made him relax. Rosa savored his contented look when she petted him. She took his hand and kissed his wrist. He gave her a knowing look; the gesture was from Duke Alexander's playbook. "The novel. Let me explain, please." He used the moment to compose his thoughts. "I rarely speak of this; in fact, I never do because it is tragic. It is my reality, and I have learned to live with it. My parents met at Donovan's Dance Studio while taking ballroom lessons. The story is that my father took the lessons hoping to meet a girl, and he did. He met my mother, and they were very much in love. They married, had a little girl, and three years later had me. When my sister, Mary Rose, was old enough to take dance lessons, they brought her to the studio. I was an active, fidgety nine-month-old, so they dropped me off with Grandpa and Nana the night of the dance recital. Mary Rose was unafraid to dance on the stage, and the night was magical. I am grateful that their last night was wonderful, as they enjoyed the show. They were so proud of her. A car accident on the way home took their lives. My mother and sister died at the scene, but my father lingered, then died a few days later. I would not have survived if I had been in the car that night."

Rosa had tears in her eyes. "I'm sorry, Alex, I didn't know."

"How could you know?" His voice wavered, and he held her tight. "My maternal grandparents were gone, so I had Grandpa, Nana, and Russ's family. I was content in grade school and didn't miss what I never had. Grandpa was my idol; we did everything together. Nana always stayed in the background and allowed me to nurture my bond with Grandpa. She must have sensed time with him would be short-lived. When I was nine, Grandpa had a heart attack and died in the hospital."

"It must have been difficult for you to go to the hospital with me, Alex. The memories must be very traumatic."

"I was upset, but knew you needed me. I had a moment of panic when you first told me about your father's heart attack. Anyway, the book comes later. After Grandpa's death, Nana suffered with grief but put her feelings aside to tend to me. My world crumbled. I didn't want to continue with Cub Scouts, basketball, or anything else without Grandpa. It was painful. Nana wanted Uncle Russel to help, but he had personal problems with his business and Russ. He couldn't devote much time to me and was grieving after losing his father and his younger brother."

"What was the problem with Russ?" asked Rosa. "He doesn't seem the type to be disruptive in school."

"Russ was a great kid, but a terrible student. I helped him with homework even though I was younger. It wasn't until his junior year in high school that his English teacher suspected he had dyslexia."

"I never would have known, Alex. Does Chrissy know?"

"He told her. He never admitted that to any other girl; he trusts her."

Rosa smiled. She knew Russ and Chrissy had something special.

"Anyway, my salvation came from a most unlikely place. The Donovans befriended my grandparents after the car accident. I called them Uncle Fred and Aunt Jackie even though they were not relatives. Nana told Jackie I couldn't sit still in school and was getting in trouble. The teacher said I had 'restless feet.' I had lost interest in everything, but Fred brought me to the studio and gave me my first pair of tap shoes, finally finding an outlet for my hyperactivity. He realized I had talent and showed me everything he knew. The studio became my second home. Little girls who befriended me surrounded me; they enjoyed the novelty of a boy in their classes. Fred choreographed several funny group dances that included me and expanded my knowledge beyond tap. I took ballet but refused to wear a leotard. Reluctantly, Jackie allowed gym shorts."

He paused. Rosa had to ask, "What does this have to do with the book?"

"You remember the novel opens with young Alexander as an orphan surrounded by women with no father figure to guide him."

"Didn't you have Fred?"

Alex grinned. "I had Fred; he was a talented instructor and a marvelous mentor for dance. He was not the best role model for a nine-year-old boy. He smoked and drank scotch, and Jackie constantly scolded him about losing money on the horses. But as a dancer, he shared everything he had with me."

"How did you get the book?"

"It was given to me much later when I was a teenager. At first, the other boys teased me and called me a fairy for taking dance lessons. My only male friend was cousin Russ. We leaned on each other because we both had challenges. When I started high school, Nana suggested I try out for basketball. I was tall, and because I played with Grandpa at an early age, I was a natural. My extraordinary strength because of ballet gave me an advantage rebounding, and I earned the respect of my teammates because I was a team player. Still, I was not one of the guys. Their locker room talk troubled me, and I remained silent. The girls they talked about were my friends at the dance school, and though I knew it was mostly bravado, it made me uncomfortable. I hated myself for having similar fantasies about a girl I liked, and I tried to talk to Fred about it. He told me I was a normal male and I shouldn't worry about sexual thoughts. He knew his chat was inadequate, so he told Nana that I needed a sex talk."

"And let me guess, Nana gave you the book."

"She did. Nana explained it was normal to feel desire, and I would enjoy sex when I was older and married. Then she gave me a romance novel. I groaned. But she insisted it was full of adventure and insights into the intimate interactions between men and women. The story included male characters, and there was an obvious contrast between the men who respected and enjoyed women and those who used them. I knew little about intimacy, and the author's descriptive and explicit sex scenes intrigued me more than the adventure. It made me dream that someday I could be close to a girl, and might even appear to know what I was doing."

"A novel approach to sex education," Rosa said with a smile. "Nana is a wise woman."

They sat for a long time. Rosa realized he had shared intimate details of his life and felt closer than ever. Alex was, and always would be, the kind, sensitive boy she met at the ranch. He was complex, though he usually kept that well hidden. Rosa was glad he had shared his feelings with her. "Alex, we could have avoided heartache if we had talked."

"Of course, in hindsight you are right, but we both keep feelings bottled up. Being a lover and companion does not mean exposing your soul. We have the most marvelous non-verbal communication; we are physical and active. When work is over, we deal with the stress of life by dancing, swimming, playing basketball, or even having sex. That's our special ingredient; an active lifestyle brings us together, and that's our way of expressing affection. I encourage students and colleagues all day and put their needs before my own. When I come home, I want to feel and not talk. I suspect you have a similar experience with dentistry."

"It's so true. The thought of being with you is on my mind as soon as I finish my workday. You must think I'm very affectionate, Alex."

"I do."

"Can you show me what you learned from those romance novels?"

"Only if you think you can handle it, Rosa."

They headed for his room. Afterward, they slept.

Chapter 41

The tap class welcomed Rosa back with enthusiasm. They practiced a recital dance, and Alex was dancing with them. The dance became more entertaining when Rosa joined them since Alex originally choreographed the dance to include a comic sequence featuring Rosa. The students loved to see Alex on stage; he was exceptional and funny. Rosa had become a popular mentor to the kids in the school. She showed them that dancing was a lifelong love to enjoy regardless of career choice. Rosa's dancing was a special treat for her parents, and they realized how happy and fit she had become since she started dating Alex.

Rosa worked on her relationship with his family. She helped Aunt Mary, Nana, and Lawrence whenever needed, always willing to offer a ride or lend a helping hand. She wanted her family to accept Alex. At first, Anita was disappointed as she wanted Rosa to marry a professional, a dentist or a doctor. But she learned to allow Rosa to live her life, and she could understand the attraction. After several visits, Anita liked him more and realized he had a charm that was hard to resist. He was always helpful and entertaining, and amused her with his blatant flattery. She suspected Alex was in love with her daughter and realized the importance of a love match.

***

The flowering trees were in full bloom, a sure sign of spring. Anita's thoughts turned to the parties she would have at the lake during the summer. Rosa suggested they hold Tammy's bridal shower at their house. Tammy's maid of honor thought it a wonderful idea. On a beautiful June day, Tammy, Carl, and Lawrence drove to the lake. Tammy had a birthday present for Rosa since she thought the party was for Rosa's birthday. Tammy was confused when she saw her Bible group, then was stunned when she realized the party was a bridal shower for her. The ladies roasted Carl as he sat by Tammy opening shower gifts, and Lawrence had the job of collecting the bows and cards. Inside, sitting at the bar, Oliver, Russ, and Alex looked at Carl with amusement until Oliver remarked how they would have their turn, and then the pointing and laughing stopped. The sun was shining, and the view of the lake was glorious; Tammy enjoyed the bridal shower hosted by Rosa and Anita.

Rosa was often in Tammy's apartment while Alex, Carl, and Lawrence were playing basketball or video games at Carl's house. Tammy depended on her for advice about the wedding. She had a powder-blue suit that she intended to wear, and she showed it to Rosa.

"Do you think I should get married in this suit?"

"Why not a wedding gown?" asked Rosa.

"I am 31 years old and had Lawrence out of wedlock. I thought a white wedding gown was mostly for young girls and fanciful weddings."

Rosa didn't want to interfere but was honest. "You have never been married before, and neither has Carl. The two of you deserve the white dress and the multitiered wedding cake if that is what you want. The tradition of dressing down is usually for older couples or second marriages."

"But what would my church group say?"

"They will say you are a beautiful bride and be pleased you are marrying a wonderful guy and sharing your life with him. Would you like to go shopping?"

"Should I?"

"Let's go now."

With Rosa's help, Tammy found the perfect tea-length dress, which was covered in lace and form-fitting. It showcased Tammy's slim figure. She looked stunning and thought the dress was appropriate. The wedding dress was a warm vanilla-white color and looked sophisticated and elegant. "Do you think Carl will like it?"

"I know Carl. He'll love it."

***

Tammy and Carl married on a warm summer day in July. Russ and Alex were groomsmen; as they ushered in guests, they broke tradition and seated guests at random. "We don't want the church to appear segregated," noted Russ. "Let's mix it up."

"It's a silly tradition anyway," said Alex. "I always thought it awkward if the bride or groom had more guests in attendance."

The wedding guests were relatives, tough-looking men in their 30s, and church ladies. Alex smiled when he imagined what the reception would be like. Lawrence looked cute in his suit, and Carl had taken a leap of faith and trusted him with the rings. Lawrence wasn't going to let anything happen to those rings. He wanted Carl as a dad and feared the ceremony would not proceed without the rings.

Friends and family were tearful when the pastor announced Carl and Tammy as husband and wife. The ceremony was touching, and they looked happy together. It would not be easy for them. It helped to be surrounded by the warmth and love of people who supported them. They seemed like an unlikely match, but on this wedding day, witnessed by friends and family, they seemed perfect together. The reception was in the church basement. The pastor looked the other way when someone brought in a cooler full of beer. They did not plan to drink, dance, or sing, but the merriment ensued, and a two-hour event turned into a four-hour party. Carl gave the pastor a generous donation for the church space as the luncheon became a raucous celebration; the bikers danced with church ladies, and everyone enjoyed the beer. Carl started the music and dancing, and Tammy thanked God for her fun-loving husband, who shouldn't fit into her church group but somehow did. Lawrence was asking for dance lessons by the end of the day, and Alex had to smile. Lawrence was a kid who had restless feet.

Chapter 42

Carl and Tammy left the reception with packed suitcases and headed for Niagara Falls. They would spend their wedding night in the honeymoon suite of a hotel in the Catskills and finish the journey in the morning. Because friends and family planned and catered the wedding, the family cleaned the lower level of the church after the reception. Many guests stayed to help, and they finished in record time. Tammy's mom took Lawrence to her house; the young man looked so exhausted she was sure he would fall asleep in the car.

Rosa and Alex were tired too, and Rosa expected they would drive to Alex's house and turn in early. But romance was on his mind. He had champagne on ice, dimmed lights, and soft jazz playing in the background. Alex was usually not romantic. He choreographed romantic dance moves that were usually diminished by a funny commentary that made it seem more fun than serious. He was in an unusual mood, so emotional and tender. She ran her fingers through his curls; he loved her touch. He treated her with reverence as if she were a delicate flower, and savored her beauty, her softness, her scent. His approach was achingly slow, but she waited. He loved her tenderly and sustained her until her last gasp of pleasure. Alex was an amazing lover. He clung to her but fell asleep, exhausted from the stress and excitement of the day. Rosa lay beside him, but was awake. She wandered into the kitchen and made soothing apple tea to help her sleep. The night had taken a serious turn and had a strange sensation of being a practice run. Practice with her dance teacher. But practice for what? Suddenly she knew; it felt like wedding night practice. Rosa realized that was exactly how she had envisioned making love on her wedding night, but decided that her imagination had taken over. Alex had not talked about marriage or the future. A few times he had made suggestions, like the night they waltzed at the showcase and he asked her to imagine him as her groom. There was the time he thought she was pregnant and told Yale they were to be married. She dismissed that as Alex being honorable and responsible. Was it possible he wanted to marry anyway? Her heart leaped with joy at the thought, but reason made her put on the brakes. Did she want to commit to him for the next fifty years? Would she outgrow him? He was a perfect boyfriend, but would he be a good husband? It was one thing to dream of marrying your dance teacher when you were sixteen. She was twenty-seven years old and a doctor with a serious job and adult goals. She had imagined marriage to be a deeply intellectual shared experience. Alex was smart and ambitious, but not someone you would say is a deep thinker or an intellectual. They didn't have serious discussions, and their companionship was based on activities. He did not seem like a soulmate. She knew in her heart she would never have a more satisfying sexual partner. Would that be enough?

She tried to calm her racing thoughts; they had not discussed marriage or children, and she put these questions aside. But he had handled her with such affection, such devotion; it seemed like he was moving beyond the boyfriend stage. She was happy now and did not want to ruin the present by worrying about the future. She decided to be content with having a perfect boyfriend. Rosa could not imagine it going any further.

***

Alex and Rosa vacationed on Long Beach Island for two weeks. Their motel room overlooked the bay, and the sound of waves against the shoreline seduced them into a restful slumber every night. They were playmates in the ocean, partners on the dance floor, and lovers in the quiet seclusion of their room. They didn't have to talk; they felt. It was the best two weeks of Rosa's life, and she didn't want it to end. Their motel room had a balcony overlooking the bay, and when they awakened early each morning, they sat there and planned their day while drinking coffee. The salt air and steady breeze greeted them as they walked to the ocean. In the evening, they viewed spectacular sunsets and enjoyed cocktails on the balcony. Privacy and intense focus on each other could get them to that mind-numbing sexual plateau they experienced the night they reunited. Rosa thought she would die if their love life had to end; the longing and attraction grew stronger as they made love more frequently. The salty air and physical exertion put them in the mood for love, and though they were not married, it felt like a honeymoon.

On Friday night, they watched fireworks on the beach. After the crowds left, they gazed at the stars and listened to the crashing waves. The moonlight glistened on the ever-changing surf.

"Did you see that, Rosa?" he asked. "It's a shooting star, make a wish."

They kept their wish private but wished for the same thing; for a future at the ocean, together, in love. It was a perfect moment, one of many with Alex, and she didn't take him for granted. Initially, they had a moment of perfection when she was sixteen. They were unsure what career they would pursue or what the future would be like as adults. He liked her when she was an awkward, skinny, sixteen-year-old. He didn't have to kiss her. But when he did, it changed her life. It meant more to her than it did to him, but he also felt the chemistry. She never knew she could want so much until she was in his arms kissing him back. A normal love story would have continued from there. There was nothing ordinary about the way they met ten years later.

Chapter 43

The idyllic summer ended too soon, and their hectic schedules kept Alex and Rosa apart for most of the work week. Rosa continued to spend weekends with him, but they never seemed to have enough time. Life became more complicated and demanding. When Tammy moved out, Alex lost the rental income, and he made less at the accounting office since he worked only two days a week. He added classes at Donovan's, but that didn't compensate for the loss. He had to make his business more profitable, and he was concerned about his finances. Rosa planned to move at the end of June because their wonderful housemate group would disperse when the lease ended. Connie and Charlie would marry that summer. Megan planned to rent the upstairs apartment from Alex. Chrissy didn't know what she wanted to do, but Rosa expected Chrissy would end up with Russ, or choose to move in with Megan. Rosa thought it would make financial sense for her to live with Alex, but hesitated to suggest it because she wasn't sure he was ready to take that step, and it seemed like a prelude to marriage. She loved him, but needed more time to make such a life-changing decision. Although she would like a roommate, she considered living alone.

Rosa tried to help Alex whenever she could. She brought groceries and made dinner; she preferred to stay home with him and only agreed to free and inexpensive excursions. She realized he was struggling. They had fun choreographing at the studio on Sundays; that was a favorite pastime that was interesting and productive. The fall was breathtaking in Northwest New Jersey, so they hiked and visited her parents' house at the lake. They volunteered at charity events with Aunt Mary and Nana. They were creative and had fun on a tight budget. Tammy and Carl had them over often, and Alex reciprocated by volunteering to take Lawrence on their date nights. Rosa and Alex both enjoyed the time they spent with Lawrence.

***

For Thanksgiving, Alex invited friends and family to his large two-family house that he occupied alone. Rosa was thrilled when her grandparents accepted the invitation, and the large group included all of their close friends and family. The turkey was in the oven, and the guests arrived early. Tammy made herself at home in her old kitchen and went straight to work. Rosa was in charge as the ladies put on their aprons and waited to be assigned a task. Lawrence cared for the birds as they nested with eggs for the second time. Rosa's grandparents, the Knapiks, enjoyed the large gathering and had no problem blending in. Her grandfather enjoyed visiting with the men, and Nana and Aunt Mary chatted with Rosa's grandmother. They spent the day without the usual holiday drama, and Carl made sure his jokes were appropriate for mixed company. After dinner, they waited an hour before serving dessert. Grandma Knapik asked Anita to take a walk with her.

Anita was nervous. She wronged this woman, who lost her son, and would have loved to watch her granddaughter grow up. Anita didn't know what she was going to say. They were silent as they descended the brick steps, then Anita suggested they take the long route around the neighborhood.

Helen Knapik was the first to break the ice.

"Anita, I am so sorry we were not there to offer our help."

Anita burst into tears and couldn't control herself. The older woman put her arms around her. When she finally composed herself, she tried to explain.

"I loved Stan with all my heart and hoped we would marry. We were kids trying to act like adults and faced an adult problem. I told your son about my condition, and we weren't sure what we were going to do. We should have asked for help. We were trying to sort it out when Stan had the accident. I was so distraught I was certain I would lose the baby, but Rosa held on. Oliver is the son of my father's business partner. He has been a godsend, a wonderful husband and father, and I love him dearly. But Stan was the love of my life. Every time I see my daughter, I think of him. I can't imagine how you suffered, but I only thought about my circumstances when I made those early decisions. I was so scared that I did what I was told. It wasn't easy. You should have been there for Rosa, and it's my fault you weren't."

"Anita, we have to look forward if we want to heal. My husband told me you tried to talk to us after the funeral. I was in no condition to talk to you. I wanted to die and spent the first few months taking sleeping pills. I'm sure they were addictive since it was hard to stop taking them. I don't know if I would have believed you if you had told me about the pregnancy. In my mind, Stan was perfect, raised as a strict Catholic, and I would not want to face the reality. I could have even suggested that some other man was the father. I don't know what I would have done. But when we saw Rosa at our doorstep, we immediately knew she belonged with us. I am so grateful for the opportunity. She is a lovely girl; you must be so proud of her."

"We are. I'm happy she has a career and hope she does it right when she gets married."

"Alex is very nice."

Anita hesitated. "We all like him, but I am concerned she will have a hard life with him. He does not seem to be a good provider."

"My husband and I have been married for over fifty years. We have a beautiful home and can spend money on anything we want. But our most precious years were the years of struggle when we had nothing but each other. Rosa has a good career and will always be able to care for herself. It is more important for her to find a supportive partner, not a rich one."

Anita shrugged her shoulders. "I guess she could be happy with Alex. He certainly has an optimistic view of life."

***

Rosa thought about Christmas. The past three had been disappointing, and her Christmas with the Dixons had been devastating. This time, her only expectation was to spend the holiday with Alex. They visited Tammy and Carl on Christmas Eve and had fun sharing the excitement of Christmas with a ten-year-old. Lawrence was ecstatic this Christmas; he had a dad. He didn't need anything else.

That night, Alex and Rosa toasted their first Christmas Eve together. The fiber optic tree reminded them of that first night together when they surrendered to each other and took a chance. The passion hadn't faded, not even a little.

In the morning, Alex made coffee and cinnamon rolls, and they exchanged gifts. Rosa was a good sport about receiving a frying pan; the gift was thoughtful since she broke the yolks when she tried to make eggs over easy. "Just what I always wanted; you are such a romantic, Alex," she teased as she eyed him in his Snoopy t-shirt and holiday boxers. His outfit was interesting. His boxer shorts said naughty and nice; naughty in the front and nice in the rear. Rosa wasn't sure what that was supposed to mean.

They cleaned off the coffee table, and she followed him into the kitchen. He looked at her and told her he had another gift for her. Because they were in the kitchen, she had wild thoughts about his intentions. But then he opened a kitchen drawer and removed a small package. The box was the right size. She lost her breath. Surely he wouldn't propose in his boxer shorts.

He did. Alex went down on one knee before her, and she looked at him in disbelief. He took her hand. "Rosa, I love you with all my heart. I want to spend the rest of my life with you. Will you marry me?"

She cried and couldn't stop. This was not the expected reaction. She was shocked and needed a moment to think. Finally, he stood up and put his arms around her. "I'm sorry, Rosa, if I misread your feelings for me."

She tried to control her trembling voice. "I didn't think you wanted to marry."

"Well, I didn't really, not yet," he admitted. "But then I met you."

She gazed at the amazing man before her. This was the most important decision of her life. She loved him, and she was happy with him. She wasn't quite ready to make this commitment, but when she looked into his hopeful blue eyes, she realized she would not disappoint him. He needed her. Rosa was ready to take the ultimate leap of faith. She was unable to speak. She presented him with her left hand, and he placed the ring on her finger; a perfect fit. They embraced. And then she had an overwhelming sense of completion, contentment, and relief. She clung to him as though she would never let go.

When she looked at Alex, she saw her handsome groom, her devoted partner, the father of their children. Alex was unexpected, but it made sense. He was the man she longed for, the only man who truly made her happy. Their Christmas Day was full of love and hope, and they couldn't wait to tell Nana and Aunt Rose when they picked them up for Christmas morning Mass.

Both ladies noticed the ring and could hardly compose themselves during Mass. They asked Father Cassidy to give a special blessing and asked questions about a wedding that Rosa and Alex hadn't had time to discuss. Aunt Mary and Nana were almost in shock. They thought Alex would give them a hint before he made this major decision, but he kept his intentions private. Carl knew since he brought Alex to his friend's jewelry store to buy the ring. The women were bursting with enthusiasm and overjoyed. Rosa and Alex had breakfast with Nana and Aunt Mary, then drove to the lake to be with Rosa's family. The ride was quiet, and Alex admitted he was nervous.

Rosa wondered how her parents would react. "Maybe I should have called them first; it would have given them time to think about it."

"Your father already knows Rosa. He's the one who told me your ring size; he said he bought a birthstone ring for you in high school."

"You asked him for permission? When?"

"He has known for a long time, and so have I. He confronted me when he realized we were having intimate relations. I was so surprised by his demeanor that I told him I wanted you to commit to me."

"Why haven't we talked about this before?"

"He told me I should not make a promise until I was ready to follow through. I wasn't ready; I had to get my life in order. Then I waited until I thought you were ready too."

Oliver knew about unfulfilled promises from Yale and didn't want Rosa to be hurt again. He may have influenced Alex so much that he was hesitant to talk to Rosa about a future together. She was glad they had her father's blessing, but her mother would be challenging. "I think Mom will need time to get used to the news. I hope she won't impose her ideas on us for the wedding."

"It will be our day, Rosa, but we should give in to some of her requests. After all, you are her only child. I have a request of my own. I don't want a long engagement. I want to get married next summer."

"I'm surprised at you, Alex; you know the Catholic Church will want us to wait a year. What's the rush?"

"I don't know. I just have this feeling we should not wait."

"You're not sick, are you?"

"No, I'm fine."

"And Nana?"

"She has heart disease, but the doctors are monitoring it and don't think she will need surgery."

"Do you have a reason?"

"No, sometimes I just have an idea I can't shake. It's just a thought."

She smiled; he wanted to marry her and was anxious. "I would like a brief engagement, maybe a June wedding? If we can make the arrangements, why not? I don't see reason to wait."

Rosa was unsure about this rush to the altar. She ignored her uncertainty as she celebrated the engagement with family and friends.

Chapter 44

Rosa could now imagine a June wedding, her handsome groom, and her life with Alex in his house. When she was in dental school, the image of her future had been flawed. She did not think she would return to New Jersey. She thought she would marry Yale. Then she thought Gerry was the perfect man, smart, handsome, sensitive, and a wonderful doctor. He was all of those things, and a marvelous friend, but she wondered if they would be content as lovers. Rosa's image of her mother was flawed; she thought of her as self-centered and domineering, but Anita structured her life so Rosa could have a home and a family. Her father, though wonderful, was not who she thought he was.

The most deceptive image was the one she had of herself. She was not English, but Cuban and Polish. She considered herself serious and destined to meet a professional man with the same temperament. But then she met this dashing womanizer, who brought out the fun and the passion within her, and he was the one she fell in love with. And once again she had the wrong image; he was not a rake or a womanizer but a kind, funny, and thoughtful guy who was unafraid to be himself.

The June wedding was a miracle. After five months of craziness, everything fell into place. They had the banquet hall, the caterer, a live band, a florist, a photographer, and a camcorder from the dance school so the reception would be on video. Rosa was unsure how Nana and Aunt Mary managed it, but the church granted them a special dispensation so they could marry in six months. They took all the required classes beforehand.

Because all the wedding arrangements were close to her parents' house, Rosa stayed at the lake before the wedding. She told Alex their honeymoon would be more exciting if they remained celibate for a few weeks. Reluctantly, he agreed.

A few days before the wedding, she spent time with her roommates and packed for the honeymoon. She was so busy with the wedding she hardly thought about her missed period and was certain it was because of wedding jitters. Just to be sure, she opened her dresser and checked the expiration date of the pregnancy test. It was valid. The result shocked her. She was in a daze when Connie, Chrissy, and Megan knocked on her door and said they were taking her out for her bachelorette party. She gave them a weary look. "Thanks, guys, but I shouldn't drink anything."

Chrissy finally asked, "Rosa, did you take the test you bought for me?"

"I did. Oh, I shouldn't talk about this; I haven't told Alex."

"Don't worry, Rosa," said Connie. "It's not what you expected, but he loves you, and a pregnancy will not alter your wedding plans. We will keep it to ourselves. Let's go out for ice cream instead."

The girls changed into shorts and ushered Rosa into Connie's waiting car. They ventured onto the Garden State Parkway, their destination a famous homemade ice cream shop at the shore. Rosa, Connie, and Megan were Jersey girls; they played in the sand as toddlers, screamed with delight as little girls as they splashed at the water's edge, and grew up on the boardwalk as teenagers, walking with their girlfriends while meeting boys who would treat them to the boardwalk rides. Chrissy found the Jersey Shore later in life when she fell in love with the beach, and that is when she fell in love with Russ. They all had fond memories of the ocean, its excitement, its romance. Rosa's bachelorette party was another memorable adventure at the Jersey shore. Someday she would take her children to the ocean, so they could play in the sand and body surf in the crashing waves, an ongoing tradition for those growing up in New Jersey. They watched the waves and the moonlight as they sat on their beach towels and spoke of their dreams for the future. Rosa spent one last night at the house and slept with hopeful thoughts and sweet dreams. Her roommates encouraged her and spoke of her bright future with Alex. Rosa would be forever grateful for their friendship and their love.

***

Rosa didn't have the heart to tell Alex, a few days before their wedding, that he was a father. He seemed so happy and carefree, and she wanted him to enjoy the moment. She felt responsible for the change in life; they had planned to wait a few years before they started a family, but she had forgotten to take her prescription more than once last cycle. She didn't expect this momentary lapse in attention would lead to pregnancy. Now they would have a short time together as a married couple before bringing a baby into the world. Alex was always so concerned about his parakeets and their offspring, she couldn't imagine how he would respond to her news. She assumed Alex would be shocked and she would have to ease any anxiety and worry. Alex was not nervous about the wedding. He allowed Rosa and Anita to do all the planning; he had already learned to say *'Yes, dear'* when asked to do an errand. He questioned her judgment only once when she asked him to keep his hair long for the wedding.

He thought about the wedding pictures. "What if we look at our wedding photos years from now and my hair is out of style?"

"Alex, twenty years from now you might not have those beautiful blond curls and will treasure the photos."

"Thanks, Rosa. What a happy thought!"

"Don't worry, Alex. You'll always be handsome. You can lose your hair but not your teeth."

An older version of Alex was Uncle Russ, who had his hair and was a handsome older man.

***

Rosa remembered how reluctant Tammy had been to wear a white dress. As she slipped on her white satin gown, the epitome of virginity and purity, she realized she was following in her mother's footsteps, knocked up while walking down the aisle. The bodice of the dress was tight and showed more cleavage than expected. She was relieved she could zip it; the gown had been a perfect fit when she tried it three weeks earlier, but it had become snug around the bustline. She picked up the white garter she was supposed to wear on her left leg. Rosa tossed it in a drawer, and she wore the red one she received at her bachelorette party. It felt a little more honest.

When she walked down the aisle with Oliver, her eyes were on her handsome groom. He was smiling, perhaps nervous, but anxious to take the plunge. The ceremony was beautiful. Tammy asked three of her choir friends to sing, and a gospel sound filled the church. Father Cassidy officiated. He was nice and gave them valuable advice.

"Don't be nervous. Try to enjoy the ceremony. Savor the moment. You don't have to remember anything unless I ask you a question; say 'yes'."

They traveled to the reception hall as husband and wife. Alex kept the wedding dance a secret since he knew Rosa would not want to rehearse. She knew how he loved ballroom and knew it would be a classic. When the band played '*Night and Day,*' Rosa became emotional. She had seen Fred Astaire and Ginger Rogers dance to it many times. It was like a dream, and Alex was suddenly the only person in the room. The wedding guests witnessed their beautiful private moment. Rosa looked over and saw Russ and Chrissy kissing in the audience. Soon it would be their turn.

Afterward, a toast. Russ gave an epic speech, unaware of the lipstick on his face. They smiled at Chrissy, who had left her mark. Alex noticed that Rosa barely touched her champagne.

"Can I get you a drink?" he asked.

"Ginger ale would be nice," she said with a smile.

As he handed her the ginger ale, he noticed the bodice of her gown. Rosa looked voluptuous. For a moment, he seemed a little peaked. But then he took her hand and kissed it. "I am so much in love with you, Rosa. I want to share my life with you and can't wait to be a father to our children."

She looked deep into his eyes. He asked if she would mind if he stepped out for a few minutes. He knew. She didn't have to tell him. She gave him a knowing nod. When he returned to the ballroom, he waved and gave Rosa a big smile. He escorted Aunt Mary onto the dance floor. Mary looked twenty years younger and probably felt like a young girl in his arms. Alex was God's gift to women, the world's greatest lover, a true prince. He was an optimist who accepted whatever turns his life took and made the best of it. He didn't falter for more than an instant when life suddenly changed. And he knew her better than she knew herself.

When he returned to her, he kissed her passionately, a binding kiss filled with love and hope. The image was clear. Her life partner stood before her; he was unexpected. They would share a unique, unconventional life near their closest friends and family. Rosa would have permanent roots and continue her career with a loving husband who was happy to stay with her in her home state. Alex found the woman he wanted to share his life with, and they would have a family. He took her in his arms and led her onto the dance floor as they waltzed into a life filled with hope, love, and adventure.

The Platinum Bicuspid

A Sneak Peek at Book Three

DENTAL TALES OF ROMANCE, ADVENTURE, AND FUN

It was supposed to be an ordinary day. When Sal awakened on a bright, brisk Chicago morning, his only concern was the root canal scheduled for the afternoon. He hated to have another root canal done, but his endodontist was young and beautiful, and he could escape into those deep blue eyes while she did unthinkable things to his tooth. He couldn't put off his appointment any longer; the tooth was throbbing.

As he strolled through his home office, he noticed a file cabinet ajar. He had not left it like that. Sal had a reason to be concerned about his personal safety and wondered who was in his office and what they were looking for. He didn't trust his business partner, Victor Volkov, and having a root canal was suddenly not the most troubling task on his schedule.

Victor was waiting for Sal in a secluded booth at the back of a crowded restaurant. Victor looked sullen.

"We have a problem, Sal," he whispered.

"Is that why we're meeting here? We usually meet at the lab."

Victor's steely gaze warned Sal. "It seems we did our last job in the wrong neighborhood. The items are hot, I'll have to hold them for a while. Word on the street is they suspect your involvement."

"Damn it," growled Sal. "I told you the job was too risky." He looked at Victor with contempt.

"My association with you is over." Victor announced. " I will settle up the finances with you later, but I can't associate with you. My advice is to get in your car and not look in the rear-view mirror."

Victor stormed out and threw a ten-dollar bill on the table for his lunch and coffee. Sal lost his appetite, but realized he should eat something. He had to be careful to avoid biting down on his sore tooth, so he ordered the soup. He finished, paid the tab, and exited the establishment with caution.

The wind was bone-chilling in February. He pulled a scarf around his face for warmth and camouflage. The busy streets provided cover, and he became an anonymous figure in the crowd. He had a sinking feeling. Was it paranoia? Sal didn't think so. Nameless, faceless men could close in on him, men hired to find him. He considered his next move and concluded that the dental office might be a safe place to hide out. The office, Dental Creations Dental Studio, was in a highrise building on Michigan Avenue. Sal cut through several shops, zigzagged his way to the appointment, and climbed eleven flights of stairs to avoid the risk of being trapped in the elevator with one of his pursuers. He cursed himself; he was out of shape, overweight, and barely made it to his destination. Sal realized he couldn't go home, or stay in Chicago, or risk getting into an elevator again. He slumped into a chair in the waiting room, stressed and exhausted. Sal's heart raced, and his anxiety was off the charts.

"Mr. Senatore, how are you?" asked Leah, the dental assistant.

"Ok," he muttered.

When Dr. Amy White entered the treatment room, she took one look at her patient and took his blood pressure.

"Mr. Senatore, are you anxious about the root canal? I promise I will be gentle, and doubt you will feel any discomfort."

"I have other things on my mind, Doc. I'm not afraid of the procedure."

"Let me take your blood pressure," she suggested. It registered high. Dr. White wondered if the toothache was the cause. " I'm going to administer lidocaine and allow you to relax for a few minutes." Dr. White dimmed the lights and reclined her patient. She spoke to her assistant in the hallway.

"Mr. Senatore has high blood pressure and anxiety; prepare the operatory for an emergency visit. We'll get him out of pain and finish the root canal at a later date when the tooth has settled down."

Leah, her assistant, was happy to comply; she had a date that night and wanted to get home. Her mind was not on completing Sal's root canal. His blood pressure was lower when Dr. White took it again. She suggested a short appointment to start the root canal and finish at a second appointment. Sal grimaced with disappointment.

"I hope to finish the root canal today," he explained. "I'm leaving town on business, and I don't know when I'll be back."

The doctor sighed. "I'll try, Mr. Senatore; the calcified distal root is an impediment to treatment. If I can finish today, it will take me more than an hour and I may prescribe an antibiotic."

"I don't care if it takes three hours, and I'll do whatever you ask of me. Please, Dr. White, this is important. I wouldn't ask if it wasn't."

The assistant set up to complete the root canal. She knew Dr. White would always stay late for a patient, who often told Leah their kindness would get them to heaven. Leah had a hot date, and getting brownie points with God was not on her mind. The process wasn't easy, but after ninety minutes of skill and determination, Dr. White completed the root canal. As she removed the rubber dam, she told Leah to go home and get ready for her date. Dr. White and Mr. Senatore were alone in the treatment room.

"Mr. Senatore, your root canal is complete, but you must follow up with a buildup and a crown. You will lose the tooth if you don't have the final restoration done."

"I promise I'll take care of it, Dr. White." He gazed at her longingly. He admired her. The root canal wasn't that bad; the worst part was sitting still with an uncomfortable box in his trouser pocket. He had to get rid of it, and he had to leave it in a safe place where it could raise questions if he was no longer around. The perfect solution came to mind. "Listen, Doc, I have a present for you."

She stared at the velvet jewelry box, embarrassed. "Mr. Senatore, that is very kind, but I can't accept a gift from a patient."

He had a twinkle in his eye and flashed a grateful smile. "Please, Doc, I don't mean nothing by it; after all, I'm a married man. It's a custom piece I can't give to anybody else."

She opened the box to reveal an upper bicuspid on a silver chain. The tooth was anatomically correct, fabricated by a jeweler who knew dental anatomy. "Where did you get this?" she asked.

"Let's just say I know a guy. The bicuspid is platinum, a precious metal."

"This is so thoughtful. Thank you, Mr. Senatore."

"Please call me Sal." He gave her a hug and lingered longer than he should have. As he approached the doorway, he looked back. Sal doubted he would see her again. He would be somewhere else, or dead. He shuddered. "Dr. White, please don't take this the wrong way, but I think you should quit this job. Word on the street is that Dr. Landry is under investigation by the Chicago police. You are young, and honest, and I would hate it if you ruined your career by your association with your boss and his practice."

Amy believed him. Suspicious of the staff and clientele since starting work at Dental Creations, she felt uncomfortable working there. "Thanks, Sal, I promise I will consider your advice."

Sal was rough around the edges, but she liked him. He was friendly and had a sparkle in his eyes that made him appear more youthful than his middle age. She feared he might be in some kind of trouble and hoped everything would be ok.

About the Author

Joanne Henning (also known as Dr. Szemboski) opened her New Jersey dental practice in 1987. Her passion for storytelling blossomed into novels that blend romance, adventure, and humor against the backdrop of the 1980s. Her titles include *'Faulty Impressions,' Deceptive Images,'* and *'The Platinum Bicuspid'.* She writes under the banner of *'Dental Tales of Love, Adventure, and Fun',* a unique series about women dentists in the 1980s.

Her books and eBooks are available at your preferred retailer, with audiobooks to launch in 2026. Visit www.dentalromancenovel.com for more information.

A note from the author: If this story brought you a smile or moments of escape, I would love to hear your thoughts. Sharing a review with your preferred retailer helps these light-hearted, dental-themed romances find readers who enjoy them most. Dentistry is key to the heart!

Made in the USA
Coppell, TX
26 June 2026

82219191R00154